CJ's fears from the past were becoming all too real.

To CJ, the plane seemed too frail to endure much more…. All of a sudden, a tremendous blow came against them, and CJ knew they were falling from the sky. The plane kept plummeting with Brad working at the controls to somehow achieve the lift they needed. Nothing worked.

"You'd better get down," Brad said with an authoritative sternness that left CJ no hope that he'd recover the descent.

CJ shook her head. This just couldn't be happening. How could God be so cruel as to make her go through it again?

"I love you, Brad!" she exclaimed, knowing that if she didn't say it now, she might never get a chance.

Brad laughed. "Now you tell me."

The mountain peaks rushed up to meet them, then something miraculous happened and Brad managed to pull them up just a bit. It was too late to keep them from crashing, but they had more control, and he banked them ever so diligently toward an open valley.

"Get down!" Brad ordered, and CJ quickly complied.

"Dear God," she whispered, "forgive me my sins and deliver us from death." Her mind drifted into the memory of another crash. "He's done us in, Jan," she suddenly remembered her father saying, just before the noise of the crash tore through the plane. *Oh God,* she thought, *I don't want to die.* It was her last conscious thought.

Tracie J. Peterson is a popular inspirational writer from Kansas. Tracie has also written eight success-ful **Heartsong Presents** titles under the name of Janelle Jamison.

HEARTSONG PRESENTS

Books by Janelle Jamison
HP19—A Place to Belong
HP40—Perfect Love
HP47—Tender Journeys
HP56—A Light in the Window
HP63—The Willing Heart
HP71—Destiny's Road
HP88—Beyond Today
HP93—Iditarod Dream

Books by Tracie J. Peterson
HP102—If Given a Choice
HP111—A Kingdom Divided
HP116—The Heart's Calling
HP127—Forever Yours
HP140—Angel's Cause
HP164—Alas My Love

A Wing
and a Prayer

Tracie J. Peterson

Heartsong Presents

To Keith and Charlene,
with thanks for tolerating my multiple calls,
teaching me about flying, sending flight
maps, and throwing in all the little extras
that made this book fun.

A note from the Author:
I love to hear from my readers! You may correspond
with me by writing to:

Tracie J. Peterson
Author Relations
P.O. Box 719
Uhrichsville, OH 44683

ISBN 1-55748-910-6

A WING AND A PRAYER

Cover illustration by Gary Maria.

PRINTED IN THE U.S.A.

one

CJ stared at her reflection in the mirror. Why did she always turn introspective in the bathroom? She reached into her purse, pulled out a compact to adjust her makeup, and grimaced. Her serious expression made her look older than her twenty-one years. Time was not her friend, she decided.

Pulling out her lipstick as well, CJ touched the Burgundy Frost to her lips, blotted the better part of the color onto a tissue, and restored the makeup to her purse.

Glacier, ice blue eyes stared back at her from the mirror, while long, coppery rings of hair cascaded from her head like a waterfall. Before yesterday, CJ had worn her hair parted on the side and straight. The thick red mass had reached nearly to her waist. Now a stranger stared back at her. Why had she let Cheryl talk her into getting a permanent?

"CJ?" Cheryl's voice called from the other side of the closed door. "Can you be free at three o'clock tomorrow for the final dress fitting?"

"Three is fine," CJ called back. She could hear her friend's voice continue on the telephone with the dressmaker. She and Cheryl Fairchild had been friends since childhood. In fact, Cheryl was CJ's best friend. Correction—her only friend.

CJ stepped back from the hotel mirror for a quick survey of her new, khaki-colored outfit. Cheryl had talked her into purchasing it, telling CJ that it complimented her skin and hair color. It reminded CJ of an outfit you might wear on a safari. With a shrug of her shoulders that sent curls bobbing and dancing, CJ reached for the handle on the door.

When nothing happened, she stared dumbly for a moment. She turned the handle again, but it wouldn't catch to open the door. Instead it turned freely. CJ pulled at the door, then pushed. Finally, she gave up and called out for Cheryl.

"The door handle is broken," CJ explained when Cheryl answered from the other side.

"It won't budge out here," Cheryl answered. "Did you lock it?"

"I suppose I did," CJ replied. "I tried to turn the handle but all it does is spin." Then a little louder and with a hint of disgust, CJ added, "Things are made pretty cheaply these days. Anything to save a buck."

"I guess I'd better call maintenance," Cheryl called. "Given the cost of everything in this hotel, you'd expect the door handles to work."

"Just get somebody up here," CJ said, starting to realize for the first time that she was trapped.

She pressed her ear against the door and could hear Cheryl trying to explain her problem, via the telephone, to the front desk personnel. Much to CJ's utter frustration, it didn't sound as though Cheryl was making much headway.

CJ felt the air grow stuffy. It always started that way. She looked around the small room. Veined-marble sink and counter, toilet, shower stall. The entire room was no larger than eight by eight. Make that six by eight, CJ thought as the walls seemed to visibly move closer together.

"No one in maintenance is answering," Cheryl called to CJ.

"What do you mean, no one is answering?" The nervousness was evident in her voice. A cold sweat dampened her brow.

"Look, CJ, just sit tight and I'll go find someone."

"No! Don't go!" CJ exclaimed.

"I can't just leave you in there," Cheryl answered. "You'll be okay. Just keep telling yourself that nothing bad can happen to you."

"Cheryl, please don't leave me!" CJ's voice was near to hysteria. She braced her hands against the door hoping to steady herself. "I don't want to be alone." The words sounded like a moan.

"Look, I've seen maintenance and housekeeping people all over this place. Someone out there will know how to help us. Take some deep breaths and get a towel wet and wipe your face. I'll be just a second. You wait right here," Cheryl insisted.

"Where did you expect me to go? It's not like I can tunnel out." CJ was beginning to feel desperate. "Would if I could, though."

Cheryl's lyrical laughter sounded from outside the door, breaking a bit of the tension. "Guess you're right. I'll be back in a minute."

"Cheryl?" CJ called, but there was no answer.

CJ returned to her evaluation of the small hotel bathroom. She wouldn't even be here if it hadn't been for Cheryl. She could still hear her friend's animated voice when she'd called to announce her arrival in Denver.

CJ leaned against the wall and forced herself to remember every detail of their conversation. She knew from experience that concentrating on something other than the circumstance at hand would help to stave off her claustrophobia.

Cheryl had been so excited that day and CJ had been more than a little surprised to hear her friend announce her upcoming wedding. Cheryl had always been the one to adamantly declare herself a most content and liberated woman. That liberation had taken a back seat, however, when Cheryl had fallen hard for CJ's brother, Curt. CJ had always hoped that Cheryl and Curt would carry through with their plans and marry, but that had been before the accident. After that, everything changed. Now, at two years CJ's senior, Cheryl was marrying a man she'd known only for a few months.

Shaking off the vision, CJ tried her best to forget. "Cheryl's getting married," she reminded herself. "If she's committed to him enough to get married, he must be special."

CJ tried desperately to remember her conversation with Cheryl. "His name is Stratton McFarland," Cheryl had gushed over the phone. "He's tall and handsome and absolutely perfect for me. He even works for Daddy."

CJ had laughed at that reference. As an only child, Cheryl had been her father's pride and joy, especially after the death of Cheryl's mother. If Stratton worked for Benjamin Fairchild and had passed his close scrutiny, he must indeed be a most unique specimen of man.

CJ felt her head begin to swim. Her cheeks felt hot, but she knew from experience that the blood was, in all actuality, draining from her face. She imagined that it pooled somewhere in the tightening ball that had become her stomach. It was, she concluded, the reason she generally vomited when the sensation of being closed in got to be too much.

She slid down the wall to crouch with her head on her knees. Her vision narrowed as the black walls inside her mind closed in.

Then it began.

At first it was just the pulsating hum of her blood, rushing to leave her head. Then it changed and grew louder. Now it was the drone of her father's airplane.

The noise increased. They were flying back from an air show in the Midwest when something happened. CJ could feel the vibrations of that fatal moment. After years of training with her father and piloting a variety of planes, she'd known instinctively that something was desperately wrong with her father's aircraft.

"We're going to crash!" she could hear her father tell her mother. The look they had exchanged put more fear into CJ's heart than she had ever known. More words were spoken, and then her father had glanced back at her. It was for only a second. He fought to control the plane and offered her a parting smile. "Better get down into position, Squirt," he'd said as easily as if he were telling her to take the dog for a walk.

"Daddy!" CJ wondered if she'd said the word aloud or if it was only a ghostly murmuring from the past. The droning in her head brought her back to reality. "I can't pass out," she moaned and slumped onto the bathroom floor.

⁂

Cheryl wasn't having any luck. In a hotel as big as this one, it seemed incomprehensible that no one could help her. She was beginning to get quite agitated when she spotted a man in coveralls and felt a wave of relief. Poor CJ would no doubt be frantic by now.

"Excuse me," Cheryl said and took possessive hold of the man's tan-colored jumpsuit.

An oil-smudged face with twinkling green eyes looked down at her. "Yes?" the man questioned.

"I have an emergency upstairs, and I need you to grab your maintenance tools. My friend is stuck in the bathroom . . .the handle broke off on the door. You have to hurry. She's got a real problem when it comes to tight spaces," Cheryl said, paying no attention to the man's surprised reaction.

Dropping her hold on his arm, Cheryl turned to punch the up button for the elevator.

"My, ah, tools," the man said with a note of amusement in his voice, "are downstairs, not up. Why don't you tell me the room number, and I'll follow you after I get my things."

Cheryl glanced first to the elevator and back to the man. Her shoulder-length blond hair flipped from side to side as she tried to make up her mind.

"We have to hurry," she emphasized. The elevator doors opened and the burgundy-uniformed operator waited for her to enter. Looking back to the maintenance man, Cheryl seemed genuinely distressed.

He smiled sympathetically. "Look, miss. I understand the urgency. In fact, I'll take the stairs down and you go ahead to your room. What's the number?" the man asked softly.

Cheryl bit her lower lip and gave in to his suggestion. "Six hundred eighteen," she answered and stepped into the elevator. "You will hurry, won't you?"

"It won't take me but a minute."

Cheryl hoped he was telling the truth. He seemed sincere enough, but she knew CJ would be half out of her mind by now. Glancing at her watch, Cheryl could see that she'd been gone for over twenty minutes.

"Poor CJ," she whispered.

❧

CJ could feel the twisted metal binding her body to the small enclosure toward the back of the plane's fuselage. She had been sixteen when her father's plane crashed, claiming both his life and her mother's. Yet in spite of the severity of their accident, CJ had never lost consciousness. She could smell fuel all around her and frantically wondered if she would survive the crash only to be consumed by a fire.

After what had seemed like hours, she could hear the

rescue vehicles screaming their way to the field where her father had fought to land the plane. More evident than any other sensation, however, was the helpless feeling of being tied to the wreckage. CJ had never been the same after the experience. Claustrophobia had emerged as the result of the crash, that and three years of rehabilitation for her shattered left leg.

Lying on the cold marble floor, CJ fought to remain awake. The flashback to the crash was so vivid that for a moment she could almost smell the aviation fuel. Curling into a fetal position, CJ pulled her knees to her chest and rocked slightly on her side. *Why doesn't Cheryl come back? Where is she?*

CJ opened her eyes for a moment, saw the room spin, and closed them tightly again.

"CJ!" a voice called to her. Was it a memory?

"CJ!" the voice came again, and she struggled to concentrate.

"Cheryl?" she asked weakly.

"Yes, it's me," Cheryl called from outside. "Maintenance is on their way. You okay?"

"I'm sick, Cheryl. You know, same old stuff."

"I know and I'm sorry. I hurried and. . ." Cheryl paused. "He's here CJ. The maintenance guy is here. You hang on. He's going to have you out of there in just a minute."

CJ forced herself to sit up. Somehow, even in her state of mind, it seemed more than a little degrading to think of the hotel maintenance man finding her on the bathroom floor. She leaned back against the wall just under the towel rack and waited.

When the door opened moments later, CJ didn't have the strength to get up. Why did she have to be such a baby about these things?

Cheryl rushed into the bathroom, pushing the bewildered man aside. "CJ! CJ, talk to me, honey!" she exclaimed.

CJ looked up and, when she did, she caught sight of the man who stood vigil in the doorway. She tried to smile her thanks, but Cheryl was pulling at her arm.

"Come on, try to stand. We'll get you out of here and get you something cold to drink. You can lie down on my bed and rest until you feel better," Cheryl was saying. "Did you hear me, CJ? Come on, help me out here."

CJ tried to stand with Cheryl's help, but her knees buckled under her, just as the maintenance man reached out and pulled her into his arms.

"I'll go turn the covers down," Cheryl said, pushing past the man. "You bring her, okay?" Obviously used to getting whatever she demanded, Cheryl left without waiting for him to answer.

"Sorry," CJ barely whispered. "It's this claustrophobia thing."

"Don't worry about it," he replied with a warm smile. "I think your friend has the best plan, though. You'll feel better after you lie down."

CJ felt her stomach lurch and knew she was going to throw up. When the man started to lift her, she shook her head adamantly. "No, wait. I think I'm going to be sick."

The man never hesitated. Pulling CJ against his left side, he lifted the toilet lid and centered her over it. CJ unceremoniously lost her breakfast while the maintenance man held back her long, copper hair with one hand and with the other firmly encircled her waist.

"What's keeping you two?" Cheryl called from the other room.

CJ struggled to compose herself and straightened up to face her rescuer. It was hard to be dignified, given her current state, and she felt like laughing for the first time since she'd arrived at the hotel. The man beside her sensed her amusement. "Just give her a minute," he answered Cheryl.

Cheryl appeared in the doorway as CJ was rinsing her mouth. She realized at once what had happened. "Oh, CJ. I'm so sorry. I forgot how badly these things affect you."

CJ was aware that the man's hands never left her. One minute they held her upright, the next they easily lifted her against his chest.

"Really, I'm much better now," CJ protested. "I can walk."

"No sense in pushing yourself," he declared, following Cheryl.

The scents of musky cologne and oil filled CJ's senses. "I'm grateful," she said, lifting her ice blue eyes to meet his warm, green ones. "My name is CJ."

"I'm Brad," he replied and deposited her on the bed.

"I'll bring you some tea to settle your stomach," Cheryl said after removing CJ's shoes and pulling the sheet up under her chin.

"Look," CJ said, propping herself up on an elbow, "I'm really sorry about this. Thank you for everything." In complete exhaustion, she fell back against the pillow and closed her eyes.

Brad stood for a moment, mesmerized by the pale-faced woman. How could two people share such a moment as they had just minutes before and know nothing more about each other than first names? Pulling the door closed, he went back to the bathroom door and began to repair the handle.

"I've called room service," Cheryl announced, coming up from behind. She peered over Brad's shoulder as if inspecting his work. "But if they don't respond any faster than anyone else does in this place, I could be married and moved out before the tea arrives."

"Having trouble with the service, eh?" Brad questioned casually.

"If I hadn't come down for you myself, I'd still be sitting here with CJ passed out in the bathroom."

"I guess I'd best let the management know," Brad offered good naturedly.

"I already plan to," Cheryl replied, adding, "Can you see to it that this doesn't happen again?"

Brad gave the perky blond an appraising glance, then winked to break the tension. "I thought it might be more to my advantage to see to it that all the handles fell apart. Then I'd have a good reason to come back and see our friend more properly. She seems to be quite an intriguing woman."

Cheryl laughed. "You certainly move fast, but you might as well save your time and energies. CJ is a wall of ice. She wants only to hide out in that apartment of hers and listen to classical music."

"Doesn't she work?" Brad questioned. He finished with the door handle and stood to receive Cheryl's answer.

"She doesn't have to," Cheryl said with a coy smile. "Bet that makes her even more attractive, eh?"

Brad didn't take offense. He picked up his things and turned at the door. Matching Cheryl's smile, he said, "Just let me know if you need anything else repaired. In the meantime, I'll let the management know about the door."

❧

Later that afternoon, a completely recovered CJ sat quietly reading while Cheryl rushed around the room and made at least fifty phone calls. When a knock sounded at the door, the two women exchanged glances.

"I didn't order anything!" Cheryl exclaimed with the telephone halfway to her ear.

"Don't worry about it," CJ said. "You just work on getting your hair appointment. I'll get the door."

CJ opened the door and found a huge bouquet of red roses being thrust forward. She immediately noted the card addressed to Cheryl and presumed the flowers must be from the perfectly romantic Stratton McFarland. Taking the flowers in hand, CJ was surprised when the delivery boy didn't wait for a tip but sauntered off down the hall.

"Wow!" Cheryl exclaimed, hanging up the phone. "Who are they for?"

"Well, who do you think?" CJ answered with a laugh. "This isn't my room."

"I'll bet they're from Stratton!" Cheryl put the flowers on the coffee table and ripped open the envelope. "Well, I'll be," she muttered.

"What?" CJ couldn't resist asking.

"We've been invited to dinner in the penthouse."

"I didn't know Stratton was staying in the penthouse," CJ said, retaking her seat.

"He isn't." Cheryl glanced up from the letter, then handed it to her friend.

CJ read the note, uncertain of what to expect:

> *The management regrets the unfortunate accident that befell you this morning. Please accept this expression of our sincerest best wishes for your speedy recovery. We would also like to extend an invitation to both of you for dinner in the penthouse suite, this evening at seven o'clock.*

CJ looked up and met Cheryl's bewildered expression. "A bit much for a broken door handle, don't you think?"

Cheryl laughed. "I can't imagine receiving this kind of welcome. Especially after all the things I said downstairs in the lobby and on the telephone."

CJ grinned. "Gave them a bit of a hard time, did you?"

Cheryl nodded. "I think dinner sounds like fun. Shall we go and let them make their apologies in person?"

"I didn't bring anything with me to change into," CJ said, getting to her feet. "I hardly think this African safari getup would be appropriate, and there certainly isn't time for me to get home and back before seven."

"You can wear something of mine," Cheryl replied.

"Your dresses are too short on me," CJ protested.

"Not my green tea-length," Cheryl said, already planning the evening in her mind. "It'll go perfectly with your hair, too."

"I don't know."

"Come on. It'll be fun. The best part is," Cheryl said, pulling CJ to the bedroom, "it'll get us out of here and give us a reason to dress up!"

An hour later, CJ appraised herself in the dressing room mirror. Cheryl was right. The richness of the forest green material clung to her in all the right places.

The sound of the telephone ringing caused CJ to abandon her examination. Cheryl was just hanging up the phone when CJ poked her head through the door. "Problems?" she questioned.

"It seems my plans have changed. Stratton has just come back to town and wants to take me out to dinner. He'll be here in about fifteen minutes."

"Oh, well," CJ said. "So much for that."

"You're still going to go, aren't you?"

"By myself?" CJ asked. "You expect me to go sit with some stuffy old hotel manager and listen to him drone on about the virtues of his resort, while you dine in the pleasant company of Mr. Perfect?"

"But it's too late for both of us to bow out gracefully," Cheryl insisted. "Just go and stay for a short time, then excuse yourself and come back here. Here, take the extra key card and wait until I get back."

CJ shook her head. "It isn't my style, Cheryl."

"Look, they're really trying to make amends for what happened. I'll bet that maintenance guy. . . What was his name?"

"Brad," CJ filled in absent-mindedly.

"Yes, Brad," Cheryl confirmed with a nod. "He probably went back to his boss and told him how you lost it and now they're worried that you'll sue them or something. Just go and enjoy yourself and accept their gesture of apology."

CJ stared at Cheryl's determined face. "Oh, all right," she finally sighed in exasperation. "I'll go."

two

CJ took the elevator to the penthouse, but only because it was glassed-in on one side and allowed her to look out on the Denver skyline. It also helped to have the companionship of the elevator's operator.

"Penthouse Suite," the operator announced when the doors opened into a brass and glass vestibule.

CJ stepped out of the elevator and glanced around hesitantly. The only way seemed to be down a short corridor to where double oak doors waited. Taking a deep breath, she walked slowly, with images of a martyr being led to her execution coming to mind. Smiling at her own misgivings, CJ refused to notice her surroundings. *The sooner this is over,* she thought, *the better.*

CJ knocked on the door and smoothed the skirt of her already perfect dress. She was still looking down when the door opened.

"Feeling better, I see."

CJ's head snapped up to meet Brad's dark green eyes. He was dressed impeccably in a navy suit. . .a very expensive navy suit. Gone were the oil smudges and grease-monkey coveralls. His brown hair was neatly parted on the side and stylishly combed back, while the sweet musky scent of his cologne wafted a greeting.

"I don't understand," CJ murmured.

"Brad Aldersson III, hotel and resort owner," he said with a charmingly boyish grin, "and occasional maintenance man." He extended his well-manicured hand to take CJ's slim arm. "Come inside, Miss CJ. . . ." He purposefully fell silent and waited for her to fill in the rest.

"O'Sullivan."

"Ahh," he replied with a grin. "Irish and a redhead."

CJ couldn't resist a smile. "Hot-headed, too. My father said it just went with the territory."

"That's all right," Brad said, pulling CJ gently into the suite. "I'm descended from stubborn Swedes, myself."

"Oh, really? Did it rub off?" CJ asked. Brad closed the door and shrugged.

"I guess I'll let you be the judge of that. By the way, where is Miss Fairchild?"

"Her fiancé called at the last minute so she had to cancel. I was going to beg off, too, but Cheryl said that would be unquestionably rude. So, here I am."

"I'm glad you came," Brad said, offering her a seat in the spacious living room. "I feel very badly about what happened to you. I pride my resorts on being first-rate."

"You have others?" CJ asked, hoping to keep the conversation steered away from anything personal.

"I have seven altogether," Brad replied. "Six are here in Colorado and one is in Jackson Hole, Wyoming. I hope to continue expanding in the future."

"How interesting."

"Oh, it can be," Brad answered. "But it's also a big headache at times. Good help is hard to get and keep. Up until two weeks ago, I had a fantastic executive assistant, but he hired on with a national chain and left me to handle my own problems."

"So here you are, trying to fix broken doorknobs and entertain claustrophobics," CJ said and laughed.

"I guess you could say that, but enough about me. What about you?"

"What about me?" CJ asked rather defensively.

Brad sensed her withdrawing a bit. "Well, why don't we start with your name. What does CJ stand for?"

"Curtiss Jenny." She said it in a matter-of-fact way that suggested everyone was named after aircraft.

"You mean like the biplane?" Brad questioned curiously.

"Exactly like it," CJ said with a smile. "My father gave it to me. When I was little, I was called Jenny, but as I got older, CJ seemed to work better."

"I love it!" Brad exclaimed, surprising CJ. "I adore the Jenny biplane, and I think it a most unique name for a girl."

"Unique wasn't quite the term my mother used. She used to say, 'Doug, you're saddling that girl with a terrible burden.' But," CJ paused, feeling a bittersweet pain at the memory of her parents, "as you can see, I fared just fine."

"I'll definitely second that." Brad couldn't resist the compliment. "Where are your folks, now?"

"Dead. They were killed in a plane crash." The pain it caused her to remember was evident in her expression.

A sudden revelation dawned on Brad. "You said your father's name was Doug?"

"That's right." CJ grew apprehensive, wondering if she should have kept quiet.

"Douglas O'Sullivan, the famous flyer?" Brad asked with a raised eyebrow.

"Yes." CJ steeled her nerves for the assault that was bound to come. It was always the same. Whenever someone familiar with her father's career found out that she was his daughter, they deluged her with questions about his life and death.

"Well, I'll be." Brad sat back in genuine awe.

CJ sat in silence. She fidgeted with the beaded cuff of her sleeve, waiting uncomfortably for Brad to say something.

"The accident was five or six years ago, wasn't it?" Brad

more stated than questioned.

"Yes," CJ replied softly. "It was five."

"The world lost a truly great man when he died. I'm not ashamed to say he was my inspiration. I started flying after attending one of his air show performances." Brad went on, but CJ barely heard him.

The same things that always crossed her mind when people learned of her true identity began to play themselves out in her head. *He knows now that I'm rich,* CJ thought. It was a well-publicized fact that she was an heiress, having inherited, along with her older brother, millions of dollars and property.

She tried to rationalize away her fears. Brad obviously had his own money or at least he had his investments in the resorts.

"CJ?" Brad quietly spoke her name.

"I'm sorry," she said with a start. "I don't like to dwell on my parents. I was just sixteen when I lost them, and it's still hard."

Brad nodded and tried to lighten the conversation. "So that would mean you're twenty-one, right?"

CJ nodded with a look somewhere between a smirk and a smile. "Think you're pretty smart, eh?"

"At least it got you smiling again. For a few minutes there, you looked too serious, almost worried." Brad noticed her discomfort. "I told Miss Fairchild, in a roundabout way, that I'd like to get to know you better. You aren't spoken for by anyone else, are you?"

Surprise registered on CJ's face. "That's a pretty straight-forward, if not old-fashioned, question to ask someone you just met. But, the answer is no. I'm not seeing anyone."

Brad's face lit up. "Good. I wouldn't want to step on any toes."

CJ shook her head. "You are a most unusual man, Mr. Aldersson."

"You aren't going to keep calling me that, are you?"

"It is your name."

"So's Brad, and I prefer we use it," he replied. "I can't imagine us getting very far, using formalities like Mr. Aldersson."

"And just how far did you expect us to get, Brad?" she asked, sizing up the man before her.

"I guess I'll leave that up to you," he answered with a sheepish grin. Strange feelings surfaced for just a moment, before CJ recovered from her surprise.

"How about something to drink?" Brad offered, getting to his feet.

CJ steadied herself once again. "I don't drink." She waited for the inevitable goody-two-shoes comments.

"Not even water?" Brad questioned in mock sarcasm.

His approach surprised CJ, but flipping her long curls over one shoulder, CJ faced the situation as she would any other battle. Surrounding herself with a wall of indifference, she spoke. "Look, I don't want this to sound presumptuous, but I would just as soon put aside any misgivings you might have."

She paused and drew a deep breath. "I don't drink liquor. I also don't smoke, dance, do drugs, or believe in having sex before marriage." She blurted the rhetoric out in the same routine fashion she'd used since finding herself on her own at sixteen.

Lowering her eyes, CJ felt almost embarrassed by her declaration. *Oh well*, she thought, *let him think me strange. I don't need him or anyone else*. Mustering her courage, CJ raised her eyes to meet his gaze. Instead of the disgust she expected, she was stunned to find his amused stare.

"You're different," he finally said with a lightheartedness that put CJ on edge, wondering what he'd say next. "And I find you fascinating."

"Most people find heiresses to be so," CJ said without thinking.

This only served to broaden Brad's smile. "Tell me, Heiress," he said with a roguishness that instantly put her off guard, "are you a Christian?"

CJ hadn't expected the question. Her mouth dropped open for a moment before she regained her composure. "Yes," she finally replied. "I am."

"That's wonderful!" Brad declared. "I am, too. Would you by any chance be interested in attending a Bible study with me? We have a great group going on at my church. We meet once a week and most everybody there is single."

"I don't know. I've not been all that interested in starting new relationships. Besides, I really don't know you," CJ stated.

Brad refused to let her withdraw. "I've never shared a more intimate moment with anyone than the one I shared with you earlier today."

CJ shook her head. "Holding someone's head while they vomit can hardly constitute the foundation for a relationship."

Brad laughed out loud. "Why don't we share dinner and stretch that meager foundation?" He extended his hand to help her to her feet. For a moment they stood facing each other, almost as if ready to step into a waltz.

Brad smiled. "Don't dance, huh?"

CJ countered his grin. "Never learned how."

"We'll have to remedy that," Brad replied.

CJ grew uncomfortable at the low, husky tone of his voice. "What's for dinner?" she asked, hoping to break the spell.

"How do you feel about Italian?"

"Love it," CJ admitted.

"Good, then what we don't eat tonight, we can take with us on our picnic tomorrow."

"What picnic?" CJ questioned. Forgetting the effect of looking into his eyes, she lifted her gaze to meet Brad's.

"The one I intended to suggest for our second date."

"I see." CJ heard her voice tremor slightly. He was too close and too impressive. She wanted to draw back her hand, but he held it so possessively that CJ was certain he'd never willingly release it.

"Does that mean you'll say yes?"

"Let me see how good the food is first," CJ said with a grin. For some reason, it all seemed very right.

Dinner proved to be wonderful, and even CJ had to admit that she was quite comfortable in Brad's company. Taking their tea with them to the balcony, CJ enjoyed the warm summer breeze.

"Do you live here in Denver?" Brad suddenly asked.

"I have an apartment here," CJ admitted. "My parents also left me a couple of cabins. One is in the Sangre de Cristo range near Westcliffe, Colorado. The other is just outside of Skagway, Alaska."

"I know Skagway quite well," Brad replied. "Wonderful town! I flew for a commuter company out of Juneau when I was nineteen. One of my regular flights was in and out of Skagway."

"Daddy loved the challenge," CJ remembered. "It used to scare me every time we made the final approach."

Brad nodded. "It was a thrill and a half, to be sure. There I was, coming down the passageway. . . ." He began one of those infamous pilot stories that always began with the three words, "There I was." He used his hand to simulate his approach. "Mountains on both sides and a narrow harbor strip to land on."

"We hugged the mountain so close on the one side that I thought I could very nearly reach out and touch the trees," CJ added. She was drawn into the story against her will. *Dear God, don't let me get sick again*, she prayed silently.

"There were times when I thought it would be necessary to do just that. You nearly had to embrace the mountain, then pull a one-eighty, turning completely back the way you'd come in, and head almost straight down," Brad elaborated.

CJ nodded. "Daddy called it wing-and-a-prayer flying."

"I remember reading that somewhere. I always liked that better than seat-of-your-pants flying. Seemed closer to God."

"True," CJ admitted. "I think that was Daddy's sentiment, as well." Somehow, sharing the memory with Brad wasn't quite as painful as she'd feared it might be. Nevertheless, the old apprehension was there, and CJ longed to change the subject. She had no desire to explain her inability to deal for very long with memories of her parents.

"It's getting late," she began and took a final drink of tea. "I think I'd better go." She started to move toward the sliding glass door when Brad reached out to stop her.

"I've really enjoyed sharing this evening with you, CJ. Will you come with me tomorrow?"

"On the picnic?"

Brad smiled. "Yes, on the picnic. I know a terrific place, and I think you'll love it."

CJ contemplated the idea for a moment. She had enjoyed Brad's company. What harm could there be in a picnic? "All right," she finally answered. "It sounds like fun."

"Great. Where can I pick you up?"

"I'll meet you in the lobby." CJ wasn't yet ready to reveal

her address to Brad.

"Okay, let's say eleven?"

"Eleven is good for me." CJ waited for Brad to open the balcony door. "Thank you for dinner. It was some of the best lasagna I've ever had."

"Mrs. Davis is a woman of many talents. It also helps that she comes from a long line of Italian cooks. I'll have her make us a special dessert for tomorrow," Brad said, walking her to the suite's double doors.

"Sounds wonderful," CJ admitted.

Brad walked her to the elevator, then lifted her hand to his lips and lightly kissed her fingers. "Until tomorrow, then," he whispered.

CJ wanted to say something, but the words wouldn't come. She felt strange emotions return. Frantically, she searched for something that wouldn't sound awkward. Instead, the elevator doors opened and she found herself stepping inside without a word to Brad. The look on his face told her that he understood. . .maybe too much.

three

The following morning, CJ found Cheryl more than a little amused at having mistaken Brad for a maintenance man.

"I suppose I should be embarrassed at all the things I said to him about the poor management and such. But in truth, I'd have probably said those things even if I'd known," Cheryl admitted.

"No doubt," CJ laughed, playing with the handle of her coffee cup.

Cheryl looked through her calendar of events. "Now don't get so wrapped up in Brad that you forget about your dress fitting. I don't want my maid of honor looking shabby on the happiest day of my life."

"I won't forget," CJ assured her friend. "Now remind me where it is I'm supposed to go."

"Designs By Christy." Cheryl pulled out a piece of paper and jotted down the address while CJ looked at her watch for the tenth time.

"Relax. It takes only five minutes to get down to the lobby," Cheryl teased, handing the address to CJ. "And I'm sure he'll wait. . .even if you're late."

CJ stuffed the piece of paper into the back pocket of her jeans. "Do you think I look okay?" she suddenly asked, surprising both Cheryl and herself.

"You look smashing!" Cheryl said, feigning a British accent. "Jolly good, I say. Just like the good old days."

CJ nodded seriously. "I've missed them. When you went to Europe and Curt moved away, I thought I'd go crazy."

It was Cheryl's turn to sober at the mention of CJ's brother. "How is Curt?"

CJ shrugged her shoulders. "Beats me. I hardly ever heard from him after you two broke off your engagement. He never calls. Never writes. I suppose someday I'll pick up a newspaper and read that he's won a Nobel prize or something. I'd be the last to know."

"Where's he living now?"

"Florida," CJ replied. "At least he was still there a month ago. I never find out anything until he's already relocated. He's lived in seven different places in the last five years."

"The accident was hard on him. It was the end of your close-knit family," Cheryl remembered. "It was the end of our relationship, as well."

CJ nodded. "Mind if we change the subject?"

"Nope. Besides, if my watch is right, you have just a few minutes to get downstairs and meet Mr. Hotel. Or should I say Prince Charming?"

CJ stuck her tongue out in feigned disgust. "I'm going to go comb my hair or whatever you do with it. I'm still not sure why I ever let you talk me into getting it curled."

"Because you needed the change," Cheryl said firmly. "You've been stuck in a rut for five years, and if I have anything to say about it, you won't be stuck there much longer."

"Well, changing my hair is one thing," CJ replied, heading for the bathroom. "Rearranging my life is totally different." She glanced at the bathroom door handle and smiled. "Totally different."

❧

Downstairs in the lobby, Brad was already pacing back and forth when CJ stepped off the elevator. He was dressed casually and holding a wicker basket.

"You look great," Brad said and added, "I hope you're

hungry."

"Starved," CJ confessed. "You'll think all I ever do is eat."

"Not with a figure like yours," Brad answered, casting CJ an appreciative once-over. He directed her out the front door where a Jeep stood ready and waiting. "Ownership has its privileges," Brad grinned and opened the car door for her.

"Where to?" CJ asked.

"It's a surprise," Brad announced and started the Jeep.

CJ realized she'd not get anything more out of him and decided, instead, to sit back and enjoy their drive. She loved Denver and lost her thoughts in the passing city streets.

"You haven't heard a word I've said," Brad proclaimed, startling CJ. With an embarrassed nod, she admitted that he'd caught her daydreaming.

"Sorry," she offered. "I got a little caught up in memories."

"Why don't you share them with me?" Brad suggested.

"I'd only bore you."

"Hardly," Brad replied. "I want to know everything about you."

"Why?"

"You're a unique woman and I want to get all the details . . .the scoop, so to speak."

CJ laughed. "It won't stop the presses, I assure you. I'm just a nobody."

"I'm just a nobody," Brad mimicked. "You've lived a lifetime of events, no doubt, following your father and mother around the world. You're no ordinary woman, CJ. You're Doug O'Sullivan's daughter."

CJ turned to size Brad up with a frown. "Is that all you care about? Is that all I represent. . .the daughter of your dead hero?" She hadn't meant to be so frank, but she reasoned it was better to be honest than hide her feelings.

"I'm sorry," Brad began, "that was rather callous and rude. I didn't mean it that way, I assure you. I just figured that you must have experienced a lot in your life because of the life your father lived. Maybe you didn't. Maybe you stayed home, safe and sound with a nanny, or perhaps you were tucked away in boarding school."

CJ smiled and instantly forgave him the indiscretion. "No such luck. I'm guilty of the gypsy lifestyle you purport me to have lived."

"You sound like it was an awful thing."

"I guess in some ways, it was. I never knew where we'd be from one week to the next. Oh, I'm sure someone had that all mapped out, but I didn't know about it."

"What did you do about school?"

"My mother home-schooled me. I never saw the inside of a classroom until I was grown." The tightening in her stomach made CJ wish Brad would change the subject.

Brad didn't sense that anything was amiss and continued to quiz her. "What was your first memory of childhood? I mean, do you have one thing that sticks out in your mind above the rest?"

"I suppose I do." CJ remembered flying with her father and forced the image away.

"Well?" Brad pushed for an answer.

Just then, as if to rescue her from having to speak, Brad screeched on the brakes to avoid running a red light. CJ was amused to find his arm shoot out in front of her, as if to offer her additional protection.

"Whew! That was a close one," he sighed. "I guess I should do less talking and more driving."

"This isn't a town to fall asleep at the wheel in," CJ quickly answered. "I remember once. . ." The words tumbled out over themselves as CJ recalled some insignificant near-miss. She was grateful to avoid thinking of her parents and hoped to keep Brad's mind occupied with other stories. Maybe he'd forget about Doug O'Sullivan and the fact that his only daughter was sitting beside him on the way to a picnic. Maybe, but not likely.

They drove slowly through the city until they were able to catch Interstate 25 north, and then the pace picked up dramatically. CJ forgot to pay attention to the surrounding scenery as Brad broke into a story about one of his resort hotels.

"You wouldn't believe the things people take back home with them. We leave the complimentary stationary, pens, coffee, and tea. We even anticipate the cheating that goes on with the wet bar and snacks. We bill them after the fact, but we always anticipate the possibility of it happening."

CJ laughed. "But I take it this involved something much bigger."

"You might say that," Brad replied dryly. "This particular time they took a huge, cherry highboy. The thing weighed enough to require two grown men to move it, and when I finally caught up with the thief, I found myself face to face with a sixty-year-old woman who told me she simply had to have it."

CJ couldn't suppress a giggle. "What was her reason for that?"

Brad shrugged and rolled his eyes. "She said it matched her own bedroom furniture and she'd looked all over for one."

CJ broke into a hearty laugh. "How did she ever get it out of the hotel, unobserved?"

"She waited until two in the morning, and then, with the help of some hired hands, moved it down the service elevator and out into a waiting truck. After that, we card coded all the service elevators."

"Did you let her keep it?" CJ couldn't resist asking.

"Yeah," Brad said with a nod. "For thirty-six hundred dollars." At this, they both laughed until CJ felt tears come to her eyes. She hadn't even realized they'd left the interstate until Brad stopped the car and jumped out.

"Well, we're here. Now, don't look up until I help you out," he pleaded, his earnestness reminding CJ of a little boy who'd prepared a special surprise.

CJ pulled her compact out of her purse and cast a quick glance at her hair. Deciding it was still presentable, she waited for Brad to open the door.

Lord, she prayed silently, *don't let him bring up the subject of Mom and Dad again. I just can't deal with it right now.* She breathed an "Amen" and tucked her purse under the seat.

Brad opened the door and offered CJ a hand out. Her eyes met his and a moment of weakness washed over her at his expression. How could anyone look at her so tenderly, so. . . well, almost like he could see clear to her soul?

"Still hungry?" he asked, and his voice was barely a whisper.

CJ could hardly force herself to speak. What was wrong with her? "Yes," she finally answered. "Did Mrs. Davis make dessert?"

"You bet she did," Brad smiled. "I know you're starving, but I'd like to show you something first. It's the reason I brought you here."

CJ realized for the first time that she had no idea where "here" really was. Looking around her, she felt a feeling of dread begin to seep in.

"What do you think?" Brad questioned. "I live over there," he continued, without waiting for her answer. "But my hangar is back here. That's where I keep my vintage biplanes. Of course, I keep a twin-engine Beech closer to the house because I use it so often. Isn't this place great?" Brad was too absorbed in the moment to notice CJ's reaction. "You can very nearly taxi right up to the front door. I'll bet your dad would have loved coming home to a place like this."

His words trailed off in her mind. CJ felt her stomach tighten. The sound of a Cessna 180 coming in for a landing behind them made her head swim with memories. Bile rose in the back of her throat.

Brad watched the color drain from her face. "CJ? Are you all right? CJ?"

The plane's wheels touching down, the engine's tireless droning, and the ominous realization that she stood in the middle of an airfield was suddenly too much for CJ.

Slapping Brad's arm away from her, she began to walk away.

"CJ? What is it?" she heard him call behind her.

She looked around her and realized that the posh airstrip had been designed to allow pilots to live in-residence where they could simply get into their airplanes for transportation, like normal folks would their cars.

"No!" she exclaimed, shaking her head. Memories of another time were everywhere. No matter where she turned, CJ faced the things she'd avoided for the last five years. Her steps increased to a run, and she lost all reasoning.

"No! No! No!" she sobbed and ran in the only direction that seemed void of life.

"CJ!" Brad easily caught up to her and whirled her around to face him.

"No!" she exclaimed and pushed away from the shock-faced man. Instantly she brought her hands to her ears, hoping to block out the sounds.

"CJ, stop. Tell me what's wrong. Talk to me!" Brad demanded, pulling her arms down.

CJ felt her knees give way. She collapsed in a heap on the ground with Brad still firmly gripping her arms. She buried her face in her hands and cried uncontrollably.

Brad could only stare in amazement for a moment. What had happened?

Reaching down, Brad gently lifted the crying woman into his arms. He cradled her against him as he might a small child and tried to soothe the obvious heartache.

"Shhh," he whispered against her ear. "It's all right. I'm here, CJ, just tell me how I can help you."

CJ gasped for air. She could feel herself growing faint. "Take. . .me. . .home," she pleaded and fell back against his arms in unconscious blackness.

four

CJ fought her way through the endless mire that held her captive. When she finally opened her eyes, she found Brad's concerned face hovering over her. His green eyes were intent on her every move.

For a moment, CJ couldn't remember what had happened. Then everything came rushing back at once. Brad was still holding her tightly, as if he were afraid of what might happen if he let her go.

CJ couldn't think of anything to say and so she said nothing. It was Brad who finally broke the tense silence.

"You want to tell me about it?" he questioned gently.

CJ stared blankly for a moment, then shook her head. "No," she whispered. "I just want to go home. I need to be alone."

"I don't think that would be wise," Brad said. Tenderly he put her in the Jeep, even fastening her seat belt before standing back. "I don't know what's going on with you, but I'm not about to let you go off by yourself. We may not be that close of friends, but I wouldn't let a total stranger wander off alone after a scene like I just witnessed."

He came around and got in the Jeep, causing CJ to turn her tear-streaked face to the window.

"Does this kind of thing happen all the time?" he asked, starting the Jeep.

Silence met his concern.

"CJ, I'm not the type to give up. You might as well talk to me and get it over with. Besides, maybe I can help."

Still, CJ refused to respond. She stared in silence out the

window, looking beyond the airfield to the distant Rockies. "I lift up my eyes to the hills," the Psalmist had said. Now CJ found herself doing that very thing. . .the same thing she'd done a million times before.

Brad drove back to the hotel in dejected silence. He wanted so much to help the troubled young woman, yet she kept a wall of protection firmly in place between them. What was it that troubled her so? When they'd first met, it was the claustrophobia and now this incident at the airstrip. What was grieving her so that she was given to these bizarre episodes?

Brad drove the Jeep under the archway and parked in the same place as before. Without a word, he turned off the engine and came around to help CJ out of the vehicle.

"Come on," he said firmly. I'm taking you upstairs to Miss Fairchild. I don't think you're in any condition to drive yourself home."

CJ wanted to protest, but in truth she couldn't find the energy for it. "Brad," she finally managed to speak.

Brad stopped and looked down. CJ refused to look at him and instead lowered her gaze to the patterned carpet of the hotel's lobby.

"I'm sorry."

"Don't be," he replied. "Just know that I'm here and I'll be happy to listen whenever you're ready to talk."

Upstairs, Brad knocked loudly on the door to 618 and prayed silently that Cheryl Fairchild would answer. Cheryl pulled open the door in a burst of energy and enthusiasm. Her face, however, dropped the animated look when she caught sight of Brad's worried expression and CJ's lack of color.

"What happened?" she questioned, taking hold of CJ possessively. She eyed Brad suspiciously over CJ's bent head.

Brad shrugged his shoulders with a look of pure confusion on his face. "I wish I knew," he answered. "I think you should put her to bed, though. She's not in any shape to drive."

Cheryl nodded. "You wait here, Mr. Aldersson. I'll be right back."

Brad paced the room nervously while waiting for Cheryl to return. He went over every detail of his actions and couldn't begin to figure where things had gone wrong. When Cheryl came through the door and closed it firmly behind her, Brad urgently asked, "Is she all right?"

Cheryl nodded. "I managed to get enough out of her to figure what happened. Why don't we sit down and talk?"

"I'd love to," Brad replied. "I have to know what I did wrong."

"It has nothing to do with you." Cheryl took a seat on the sofa and waited for him to join her. "In fact, if CJ hadn't agreed to my telling you, I wouldn't be talking to you now. She's a very introverted, private person. She always has been, but even more so after the accident."

"Telling me what? What accident?" Brad questioned.

"The crash that took her parents' lives."

"I never thought about it," Brad admitted. "Do you mean to tell me that she still isn't over it? Was it the airfield that upset her so much?"

Cheryl nodded. "CJ's never been the same. Even though the crash took place five years ago, she can't talk about it and she can't handle anything to do with flying."

Brad rubbed his chin and shook his head. "I never for one minute intended to cause her pain."

"She knows that, and so do I."

"Please call me Brad," he urged. "I guess I knew that CJ's father was killed in the crash but, until she mentioned it,

I didn't remember that she'd lost her mother, as well."

"That's not the half of it," Cheryl admitted. "CJ, herself, was on that flight. They were coming back from an air show in the Midwest."

Brad's head snapped up and met Cheryl's worried expression. "She was on the plane when it went down? I've seen pictures of the wreckage. How could anyone have lived through that?"

"She was the sole survivor," Cheryl replied. "She was conscious the whole time and pinned in the wreckage for hours. They eventually had to cut her out in order to take her to the hospital. She very nearly lost her leg, but they managed to piece it back together after several surgeries. Then, years of rehab followed in order to get her walking again."

"No wonder she never learned to dance," Brad muttered.

"What?"

"Oh nothing," Brad said, meeting Cheryl's eyes. "Go on. What else happened to her."

Cheryl seemed to relax. "It was the hardest thing I've ever seen anyone bear. A shattered leg, multiple injuries, and the realization that both of her parents were dead. She couldn't deal with the knowledge that she'd been left behind. She hated the fact that she was still alive.

"Then the reporters and FAA people came. They drilled her for information and hounded her relentlessly until her brother, Curt, arrived and drove them off. CJ wouldn't speak to anyone, not even me. That went on for several weeks, and the doctors began to worry that maybe she couldn't talk. They thought perhaps it was hysterical laryngitis or something like that. Then one day, CJ announced to them all that she'd simply had enough and wanted to be moved from the hospital immediately. Curt arranged for her to convalesce at home, and that was that."

"She never told me," Brad said softly.

"No," Cheryl admitted, "she wouldn't. That would require facing the problem, and CJ hasn't begun to do that. It's something that has worried me greatly over the years. In fact, I have to confess that I spent a lot of time abroad because I couldn't handle the situation here at home. It came between us in a big way because I wanted to force her to deal with it and CJ absolutely refused to consider the matter at all."

"But she'll never be free of it if she doesn't try."

"I'm not sure she wants to be free of it, Brad. Although she can't face her memories, they are, as far as CJ is concerned, all she has left. She has a storage unit filled with memorabilia and family mementos. Curt and I tried on several occasions to get her to bring the stuff home or get rid of it, and CJ acted like we were both off our rockers. Curt finally gave, up and moved off, and I guess in my own way, I gave up, too."

"But all we did was visit an airstrip. It wasn't even a place she'd ever been with her parents. It's a relatively new area—"

"But don't you see?" Cheryl interrupted. "It doesn't matter! She can't even fly on a commercial airliner. CJ turns the TV off if there's an advertisement for flying. She won't visit a travel agency or go to movies or the mall—all because she's afraid she might have to encounter something to do with flight."

"But she's a grown woman. Surely she sees the need of getting past this thing. There are counselors who could help her," Brad protested.

"You have to want to be helped, Brad, and CJ doesn't want to be helped."

"Maybe I can help her," Brad said with a new resolve. He was beginning to formulate an idea in his mind.

"Would you risk being responsible for sending her into

complete seclusion?"

Brad's shoulders slumped. "What do you suggest? I can't just leave her alone."

"Just be yourself. Show her that you care, in spite of her trauma, and let nature take its course."

"Cheryl," he paused, "may I call you that?" She nodded and he continued. "I don't mean to seem harsh, but isn't this style of ignoring the problem the same thing that everyone else has already tried? It obviously isn't working."

"No, it isn't working." Cheryl's voice betrayed her anguish.

"Then doesn't it stand to reason that someone has to make her face up to the problem?"

"I don't know," Cheryl answered honestly.

"Look, I have a friend at church who happens to be a counselor. Maybe he'll have some ideas." Brad got to his feet. "I really appreciate your taking the time to explain this to me. I know God can get CJ through this."

Cheryl shrugged. "He doesn't appear to be too concerned at this point."

Brad turned in surprise, but said nothing. *One problem at a time*, he told himself. *One problem at a time.*

❧

CJ had no intention of falling asleep. She hated to sleep because when she did, the old dream came back to haunt her. Always, she was falling. Falling and falling, as though it would never end. It was always the same. Always the crash. But, to her surprise, when she awoke two hours later, she felt much better. She hadn't dreamed the dream. Instead, she had the vaguely familiar sensation of being held in warm, masculine arms.

All at once she remembered Brad. No doubt he'd be long gone after having to face two episodes of her inability to cope with the past.

Getting out of bed, CJ walked calmly into the living room and confronted her friend.

"How did it go?"

Cheryl looked up from the list of wedding guests and eyed CJ suspiciously. "Are you sure you ought to be out of bed? Brad said you had a very nasty spell."

"I did," CJ conceded. "But I'm better now, and I need to get home. Did you talk to Brad? Did you tell him everything?"

"Yeah, he was really worried about you. I don't think you've heard the last from him."

"Well, I'd be surprised to learn that he wanted to go another round with me," CJ replied, searching the room with her gaze. "Do you know where my purse is?"

"No. I didn't see that you had it when Brad brought you in. Do you suppose it's still in his car?"

"That'd be just my luck," CJ replied. "Oh well, I'm not going to worry about it. There wasn't much of anything in it, and my license is in the car. I guess I'll manage."

"But what about the car keys?" Cheryl asked, getting up to walk CJ to the door.

"I used the valet parking," CJ answered. "They have my keys."

Cheryl nodded, then reached out to touch CJ's arm. "Are you sure you can drive home?"

"Stop worrying, Cheryl. It's a car, not an airplane."

five

Brad's interest in helping CJ didn't wane with the consideration that he was really getting into something about which he knew little. He prayed in detail for the wisdom to deal with the matter and asked God over and over to show him what direction to take in order to be a help and not a hindrance.

He called Cheryl the very next day to inquire about CJ's recovery.

"She was fine, Brad. Drove herself home and everything," Cheryl answered in a distracted voice.

"I want her address," Brad suddenly said. "I checked with directory assistance for a phone number, but it's unlisted. Can you help me?"

"It wouldn't be right to give it to you without CJ's permission."

"Look, I promise I won't go over there, I just want to send her some flowers, maybe a letter or card. Please, Cheryl."

Cheryl felt torn. The man obviously cared, and it wasn't like he was some kook off the streets. Her loyalty to CJ was fierce, however, and won out. "I can't."

Brad's exasperated sigh filled the receiver. "I know she'll never call me."

"She will if she wants her purse back," Cheryl said, still wondering how she could help Brad without betraying CJ.

"What?"

"CJ think she left her purse in your Jeep."

"I didn't see it anywhere," Brad said. He tried to remember what CJ had done with it when she got in the car.

"All I know is, when she got ready to leave here yesterday, she told me she'd probably left her purse in your Jeep."

Brad smiled for the first time that day. "I'll find it, Cheryl, and I'll see to it that it makes its way home."

"Brad, please be careful. CJ is precious to me, and I won't stand by and see her needlessly hurt."

"I won't hurt her," Brad promised. "At least not the way you're implying. I want to see her beat this phobia of hers. I want to get to know the real woman inside and clear out that scared, sixteen-year-old girl. It might be a bit painful, but in the long run, CJ will be better off for it.

"Look, I'll send a bonded courier over with her purse and I'll attach a letter to it. Is that acceptable?"

"Of course. I guess it's perfectly logical that you were bound to find the purse sooner or later. I just don't want CJ thinking that I betrayed her."

"She'll never know that you even mentioned it," Brad assured. "You have my number, so don't hesitate to call me if I can be of help."

&

Over the next few days, Brad tried to get some kind of response from CJ. He had the courier require a signed receipt for the purse and letter—and the receipt was returned to him the same day—but there had been no other response.

Then he went to work trying to woo her with gifts. He'd sent flowers, balloons, stuffed animals, and candy, but they were consistently refused and returned with the delivery man back to the shop of origin. Next, he tried overnighting and same-day-delivering letters and cards, still without a single response or acknowledgment. At least they weren't refused. Finally, Brad decided enough was enough. Picking up the phone, he dialed his friend, Roger Prescott.

❧

CJ nervously paced her apartment. Why wouldn't Brad just leave her alone? She'd refused his gifts and the stack of unopened letters sat on the entryway table as evidence that she wasn't the slightest bit interested in what he had to say to her. But she was. At least a hundred times a day, she had to force herself not to open the envelopes.

He'll either feel one way or the other, CJ told herself. *Either he'll want to draw me out of my shell or he'll want to pursue a relationship in spite of it.* Neither one seemed acceptable.

"I've tried to be a good person," CJ reasoned aloud. Since her parents' deaths, she had convinced herself that accepting Christ as her Savior was simply not enough. She had deemed it necessary to be as perfect as she could in order to go to heaven. But in this situation with Brad, she felt she was failing miserably. She wasn't being good to Brad. She wasn't even being kind.

When the doorbell rang, CJ was certain it would be yet another of Brad's deliveries. She glanced down at her striped top and navy shorts with indifference as she opened the door to her apartment.

CJ's eyes widened at the sight of Brad Aldersson on her doorstep. "Brad!" she exclaimed and stepped back a bit. "What are you doing here?"

"You wouldn't call me," he offered to begin with, "and I was worried. I brought a friend with me, and I thought you might like to talk to him, since you don't seem inclined to talk to me."

CJ shook her head. "I don't need to talk to anyone."

"CJ, please just listen to me for a minute," Brad pleaded.

"I know the letters may have sounded a bit forward—"

"I never read them," CJ interjected. Brad's eyes registered disappointment, but he refused to give into it.

"Then I guess I really need to start from scratch," he continued. "My friend is a Christian counselor from my church. Roger, this is CJ O'Sullivan. CJ, this is Roger Prescott."

CJ only stared at the man's extended hand.

"I'm glad to meet you, CJ. Brad tells me that you're a sister in the Lord."

CJ didn't dare be rude with a man of God. "Yes," she finally answered and reached out to shake Roger's hand. She glanced hesitantly at Brad and then again to Roger. "Won't you come in?"

"Are you certain that you want us to?" Roger asked. "We aren't about to barge in, if you'd rather we leave."

"No, it's all right. I don't know for sure what Brad hopes to accomplish here, but I won't be inhospitable."

"May I call you CJ?" Roger asked informally.

"I suppose so," CJ replied in an agitated manner. "Won't you sit down?"

Roger shook his head and turned instead to Brad. "Brad, I know that you want to help CJ, but if it's all right with her, I'd like to talk to CJ alone."

Brad looked stunned but nodded his cooperation. He turned to meet CJ's eyes. "I would like to call you sometime," Brad said softly as he turned to leave.

CJ hated the pained expression on his face. She knew she'd caused it with her cold-shouldered attitude. "Do you have the number?" she asked.

"No."

"I won't promise anything," CJ announced. She jotted down her number and handed it to Brad. "But you have my permission to call."

six

CJ listened in awkward silence as Roger Prescott explained the role he would like to have in CJ's life.

"I know this is all very strained, and I must admit I don't usually make this kind of house call—"

"But Brad was no doubt very persistent," CJ interjected.

Roger smiled. "Yes, as a matter of fact, he was."

"He can be like that, at least from what I've seen."

"He just cares, CJ. I'm convinced that he's genuinely concerned for your welfare and that he has a deep desire to get to know you better."

"I understand that," CJ said firmly. "What I don't understand is why he feels he has to fix me. I'm just fine."

"You know, CJ," Roger began, "many times people find that they can't deal with things from their past. The mind shuts out the horrific. Psychologists once tested people by showing them pictures of Nazi concentration camps. The photos explicitly revealed hundreds of the innocent dead. After viewing the pictures, people were asked to write down one thing they remembered in particular. More often than not, what those people wrote had nothing to do with the atrocities they'd witnessed in those pictures.

"Usually," Roger continued with a soft expression of compassion, "people noted some unusual thing that had nothing to do with the death and destruction. Some noted the existence of words or markings on the buildings. One photo prompted a common response from people as they noted a child's single shoe lying in the mud. They couldn't

46

handle the scene of the dead child in his mother's arms, right beside that shoe. Their mind picked out something neutral and refused the rest."

"I don't understand what this has to do with me," CJ replied defensively.

"When faced with monumental ordeals in which the mind finds itself having to register unpleasantries or even horrifying situations, we do what we must to protect ourselves. In your case, if I understand correctly, you had to endure a tragic plane crash. The crash resulted in the deaths of your parents and injury to yourself. Now, you find that even the association of things related to flight and the lifestyle you knew before the accident are unbearable. Is that a fair assessment?"

"It hurts too much."

Roger nodded. "Yes, I know. But CJ, if you don't deal with this now, it will continue to hurt you over and over again. You must realize that burying your pain and suffering over all these years has resulted in a deep-rooted fear."

"I'm getting by," CJ replied and hugged her arms to her chest.

"Getting by isn't always enough. Is that all you want for your life?"

CJ looked up at the ceiling, refusing to meet his eyes. "It's not a matter of what I want," she whispered. "It's all I can handle."

"I'd like to help you handle it in another way," Roger said evenly. "Brad would like to help, too. You know, he thinks quite highly of you."

"No, he thinks highly of Doug O'Sullivan, my father," CJ said, snapping her head back down. "I'm just the left-behind daughter of Brad's hero."

"Brad came and talked to me extensively," Roger continued.

"At first, I point-blank refused to become involved. Like I told Brad, a person has to want to be helped. Otherwise, it isn't help, it's interference and accomplishes absolutely nothing. Sometimes it hurts the person even more."

He paused and looked at CJ sympathetically. "However, I've known Brad for a long time, and the more he talked, the more I could see the genuine concern and respect he held for you. CJ, he never once mentioned your father, except to say that you two were very close and that he'd died in the crash."

CJ got to her feet, unable to sit still any longer. She paced out a few steps in front of Roger and turned. "I was left a small fortune," she confided. "In fact, it wasn't that small. My brother and I are well-set financially and, unfortunately, this has made me a very popular woman. The first time any man learns of my true identity, he usually starts seeing dollar signs. Add to this my determination to do what is right in the eyes of the Lord and, all of a sudden, the simplest relationship becomes impossibly complicated."

"And you think Brad is after your money and that his only other interest is a kind of far-off hero worship of your father?"

Again she paced. "I don't know. I really don't know!" Her auburn hair whirled around her face as she turned on her heel. "Why does he have to care so much? He doesn't even know me. I threw up while he held me over the toilet. Then I broke down in complete hysteria when he tried to take me on a picnic. How can he possibly care whether I deal with this issue or not?"

"So you realize there is an issue to deal with?" Roger questioned gently.

CJ froze. Her face contorted into several expressions before her protective mask went back into place.

"CJ, no one is trying to hurt you or use you. We only want to help. I'm offering to set aside counseling time for you, if you want that help. And I've a feeling Brad is offering much more than that. Are you so confident that you can make it through this without help? Is there never a time when the demons haunt you so severely that you just want out?"

CJ's eyes registered acknowledgment. "How could you know?"

Roger got up and walked to where CJ stood. "It's my job to know, for one thing. For another, we all have our demons to contend with. Christ told us it wouldn't be easy here on earth. But CJ, Christ overcame the world and He's already dealt with this problem, as well. He's given you a path to find the way home. It's up to you to set your feet on the trail."

CJ nodded slowly. "It's so hard," she whispered faintly.

"I know. But you have people who care, and you don't have to walk that path alone. You have a Savior Who loves you and Who will always be with you. Even when times get rough and things are as bad as they can be, you won't be alone."

Rogers words permeated the hard façade CJ had lived behind for five years. By listening to the things he had said, CJ recognized the truth and realized that God had brought her to a very important crossroad.

"I'll think about it, okay?" CJ said with tears in her eyes.

Roger handed her his card. "Call me any time. Oh, and on the back is Brad's number. I think he'd like to know that you aren't angry with him." CJ took the card and nodded. She had a great deal to consider.

❧

Sitting in his Jeep, Brad waited impatiently for Roger. He'd wanted to be there. No, the truth was Brad wanted to be the one to whom CJ talked. He gripped the steering wheel, then released it, wishing he could feel at peace with what he'd done. In his mind he kept seeing CJ's frightened expression.

"Why can't this be easy?" he questioned with an impatient fist to the steering wheel.

After nearly an hour, Roger reappeared in the parking lot and made his way to Brad's Jeep. When he got inside, he smiled.

"I think we made a bit of progress," he said confidently.

"You honestly think so?"

"I can't be certain, but I believe CJ is ready to deal with this thing. She needs some time to think, but I left her my card and told her to call me any time and that I'd set up appointments to counsel her. I also left her your phone number. I knew you wouldn't mind."

"Of course I don't mind. I want to help her," Brad said sharply.

"I know. So do I. But we see only a little bit of the picture that makes up CJ O'Sullivan. God has the blueprints, and He's the One in charge. We must take our direction from Him or we'll only be interfering with His plan."

Brad slumped back in the seat in complete dejection. "I've never been one to just sit back and do nothing."

"I don't expect for you to do nothing. You have access to information about CJ and her family. Do a little research and learn what you can. Pull out books, newspaper articles, whatever it takes, and learn about her. The more you know about CJ as a child before the accident, the better you can help. The accident forever changed her life. She not only lost her parents, she also lost a part of herself when that plane went down. If she lets you in her life, you might be the one to help her recover that."

"I'll get right on it," Brad said with renewed hope.

"Oh, and Brad," Roger said as he fastened his seat belt, "spend a good amount of time in prayer, as well."

Brad smiled. "Of course."

❧

Almost a week later, the telephone on Brad's desk in the penthouse began to ring. Brad picked it up absent-mindedly, his eyes still focused on the column of figures before him.

"This is Brad Aldersson."

"Brad, it's CJ."

The feminine voice brought Brad's full attention to the call. "CJ? How are you?"

"Better, I think."

"Good," he replied. "I've been worried about you."

"Why?" CJ asked without thinking.

"Because I care."

"Why?"

"Do I have to have a reason?"

"I guess not." CJ paused. "Look, this isn't why I called."

"Why did you call?" Brad questioned, almost afraid of the answer.

"Actually, I wondered if you could come over and talk. I'm not good at explaining myself under any circumstances, but on the phone, I'm even worse."

Brad could hardly contain his excitement. He fought to speak evenly. "Of course. When?"

"Whenever is convenient for you."

"I'm free right now. Is that too soon?"

"No. Now would be fine. Do you remember the address?"

"I certainly do. Would you like me to bring anything? Mrs. Davis has been working up a feast in the kitchen. I could pack some of it up and bring it along."

CJ laughed, and the sound was like music to Brad's ears.

"You know me and food," she answered. "Bring whatever you like, and I'll scout around in the refrigerator and see if I have anything appropriate to add."

"Don't you dare," Brad replied. "I owe you this meal. I'll bring everything we need. You just sit tight."

CJ hadn't long to wait. When she opened the door, she burst out laughing. Two large grocery sacks with legs sticking out from beneath stood at attention. "Is that you, Brad?"

The deep chuckle from behind the food told CJ it was. "Mrs. Davis got a bit carried away, but I think you'll be pleased."

"Well, come on in. You can put the stuff in the kitchen or on the dining room table, whichever you prefer."

"Do you want to eat while we talk?" Brad questioned.

"That'd be good. At least if things get bad, I won't miss out on dinner again."

"Then lead me to the dining room table and we'll just lay all this food out," Brad directed. "Then, if you'll get some plates and silverware, we should be ready to eat."

"Okay, right this way," CJ replied and led Brad to her small but neatly ordered dining room.

Placing the sacks on the table, Brad looked at CJ for a moment. Self-conscious of the attention, CJ glanced down. "I'll get the dishes," she finally said. "Is tea all right to drink?"

"Tea sounds good to me," Brad answered.

CJ quickly retrieved the pitcher and brought out a woven bamboo tray from under the sink to put it on. She pulled down her everyday dishes and pale blue glasses and went to the silverware drawer to finish out the setting.

Taking a deep breath, CJ walked back into the dining room, carrying the tray. Brad looked up and smiled.

"Everything's ready here."

CJ noted the table and gasped in surprise. "There's enough food here for an entire dinner party."

"I wanted to make sure you had a choice. I still know so very little about you. I wasn't sure what you liked," Brad offered.

CJ looked the food over and laughed. "I don't see a single thing here that I don't like," she said good-naturedly and took the seat that Brad offered her. They were rapidly running out of idle chatter.

Taking the place across from her, Brad stared deeply into her blue eyes. "Thank you for asking me over," he said in a tone that left no doubt as to his pleasure in the matter.

CJ nodded and dropped her head in embarrassment. But the thought of praying came to mind and she quickly covered her discomfort by suggesting they offer thanks.

"Would you say the blessing?" she whispered in request.

"Of course," Brad replied and bowed his head. "Father, I thank You for this day and the meal we are about to share. I ask Your blessing on the food and those who partake of it. Amen."

CJ filled her plate in silence, knowing that Brad was waiting for her to say something to start them off. Finally, she choked back her discomfort and spoke.

"I guess I owe you a bit of an explanation, if not an apology."

Brad shook his head. "No apologies are necessary."

CJ folded her hands in her lap and looked at the food on her plate. "I know Cheryl told you about the accident. I'm certain that beyond that, given your love of my father, you must have read about it, as well."

Brad nodded, and CJ continued. "I don't remember a lot about the actual crash. I do remember being pinned in the wreckage and feeling so helpless. There was fuel everywhere," she said, remembering the smell. "I just knew that at any minute the whole plane would burst into flames. I don't remember seeing my parents, but somehow I knew that they were dead. Don't ask me how. I just sensed it, I guess." CJ fell silent, wondering if it had been such a good idea to have this talk, after all.

"You don't have to push yourself, CJ. It's good that you're willing to deal with it at all."

"I know," she answered softly. "I know that you and Roger want to help me, and I do appreciate that."

"But. . . ," Brad interjected.

CJ looked up and met his dark green eyes. "But I'm not sure I'm up to the task. I've thought a lot about what Roger said, but I don't feel comfortable going to a stranger and baring my life."

"What about me?" Brad questioned.

"You're nearly as much a stranger as he is," CJ responded.

"And do you want to keep it that way?" he asked.

CJ found his eyes fixed on hers. They held her captive in a way that was not at all unpleasant. "I'm not saying that," she finally answered. "I'm just saying that I don't know what I want. I've been chained to these emotions and problems for so long, I'm not sure I can break away from them. Or," she added in a barely audible voice, "that I even want to. Does that sound horrible?"

"Sometimes the things that bind us feel almost comforting," Brad said in a knowing way. "Kind of like the evil we know is better than the evil we don't."

"I suppose that's what I mean," CJ said, lowering her eyes once again. She toyed with her fork for a minute before adding, "I guess it just comes down to the fact that I'm afraid."

Brad reached out and stilled her restless hand. "We're all afraid at one time or another. But, if you'll let me, I'd like to be there for you. I want to help."

"Why? I don't understand how you can just walk into my life from nowhere and want to help me. I'm nothing to you."

Brad tightened his hold on her hand. "I can't explain it all. I don't know for sure why you've come to be so important to me. Maybe it's just that I don't like to see anyone hurt as much as you are. Maybe it's because you seem so lost and scared. I don't know. All I know is that I want to help. I want to get to know you better. Will you give us a chance to be friends?"

CJ swallowed the lump in her throat and fought back the tears that threatened to spill. It was the moment she knew would come. Could she make the right decision? Could she put aside her fears and break the chains?

"I'd like very much to keep seeing you," she finally managed to whisper. "Is that enough to start with?"

Brad smiled. "You bet it is."

seven

Brad fairly soared on wings of his own. He went straight to Roger's house after leaving CJ and explained her acceptance of his help.

"What do I do now?" Brad questioned, as Roger set a cup of coffee in front of him.

"You must earn her trust," Roger answered, taking a seat. "She doesn't know you, and you really don't know her. Establish a friendship, first and foremost. And," he added in a stern tone, "I mean friendship. Don't try to fall in love with her or make her fall in love with you. That would be disastrous. You need to be friends first. I can't stress that enough."

Brad took a long drink of the steaming black liquid. "I'm already drawn to her physically as well as emotionally," Brad admitted. "I may have already lost my heart to her."

"No," Roger stated firmly. "You feel sorry for her. You have sympathy for her plight and you care about her recovery. You aren't in love with her; you're merely a concerned observer at this point."

Brad grinned and put the cup on the table. "Keep talking. Maybe you'll convince me."

Roger shook his head. "Brad, this is most serious. I know it's hard, but you need to find a common ground with CJ that doesn't revolve around a physical attraction. Bring her to church. Take her to the Bible study. Offer her friendship, but don't get physical. You'll never be able to help her objectively if you do."

"I don't think I follow you," Brad confessed.

Roger leaned forward. "If you fall in love with her, you won't allow yourself to cause her pain and, unfortunately, most healing starts with that very thing. If you fall in love with her, you will only build her a bigger wall. You will convince yourself that you can keep her from the pain of the past and then she'll never deal with it. Do you understand?"

Brad frowned. He did, indeed, see the logic in Roger's words. Not that he wanted to. Much to his disappointment, Roger's advice held that solid foundation of truth that Brad couldn't ignore.

❧

CJ wasn't at all sure what to expect when Brad suggested she come to his penthouse at the hotel. She weighed her options carefully and finally accepted, realizing that she had agreed to take on his help.

She lingered in the corridor outside the penthouse, studying the brass and glass fixtures and objets d'art. Plush, mauve carpeting seemed the perfect balance to the entryway. It was refined, but not overdone. CJ ran her hand lightly across the frame of a Renoir replica. It was a painting she'd always enjoyed. DÉJEUNER DES CANOTIERS—THE LUNCHEON OF THE BOATING PARTY was printed in bold letters on the plaque at the bottom. She stared for a moment at the painted figures.

There were men in straw hats and a red-haired woman, cooing at a fluffy dog. The table was set for the luncheon, the wine goblets just catching the light. CJ's eyes were drawn to the woman in the background. She leaned casually against the railing, listening or pretending to listen to the gentleman in front of her. CJ thought perhaps she was daydreaming. Of all the characters there, the leaning woman was the one most distant. She was a part of the boating party, yet she was alone. It was almost as if the woman observed what was going on around her without truly being a part of it. It reminded CJ hauntingly of herself. Shaking off the sorrow, CJ knocked on the door.

Brad opened it and smiled broadly. "Come in. Come in." CJ returned his smile with timid warmth. "Have you eaten yet?"

"Yes," CJ replied and nervously plunged her hands into her skirt pockets. Would there ever come a time when she could face Brad with an emotion other than dread?

"There are some things I wanted to say," Brad began, "and I thought perhaps it would be best to say them here."

"I see."

"Why don't you make yourself comfortable," he motioned to a chair. "I want to say up front that I want to help you just because I care about you. It doesn't have anything to do with your father, and I don't expect anything out of it."

CJ's brow furrowed. "Be real, Brad. Everyone expects something. No one does anything without anticipating an end result."

Brad nodded. "Maybe I should reword that to say your welfare is my uppermost goal. If you are better able to deal with life and can put the pain of your past behind you, then I will have accomplished what is most important to me at this point."

"I see. A real humanitarian, eh?"

"CJ, I can't honestly say why it's so important to me," Brad admitted. "But from the moment I found you cowering there in Cheryl's bathroom, it seemed overwhelmingly necessary to be a part of your life. I propose friendship. Nothing more. Nothing less. I won't overstep those bounds, at least not until you progress to the place where you feel comfortable considering such a thing."

"Is this Roger's idea or yours?" CJ questioned.

Brad smiled. "I have to admit it was Roger's at first. But I quickly saw the logic and reasoning in what he suggested. I can't be objective if I fall in love with you." His green eyes were intense.

"Go on," she whispered.

"It's just that I want everything to be on the level with you. Roger says trust is the most important element in our beginning a friendship. I figure, first of all, that you have to feel confident that I'm not after your money or your body. I've made arrangements for my business office to open its books to your scrutiny."

"Brad, that's hardly necessary," CJ protested. She was touched that he would do such a thing, but it embarrassed her greatly for him to think her so insecure about her money.

"I insist. This is one matter in which I won't take no for an answer," Brad stated firmly. "Another area I insist be clear between us is that any time you feel I'm moving too fast or expecting too much, I want you to tell me so. I'm not porcelain, and I won't be hurt. I promise."

CJ smiled at his insistence. "All right," she agreed. "But I have some demands of my own." The words surprised CJ. In all honesty, she hadn't considered such things until just then.

"When you check in with Roger for advice on how to help me, I want to know what he says. Just because I don't feel comfortable enough to see him on my own doesn't mean I want you two discussing me behind my back. I'm willing to try and deal with this thing, but I've never held much store in shrinks. That goes for Christian ones, as well. Fact is, I've always thought the two things kind of conflicted with each other. But that's another issue. Do you agree?" CJ asked.

"Agreed. It's only fair that you know what advice Roger

offers. In fact, we can discuss that right now, if you like."

"All right, what does the good doctor say?"

Brad grew serious. "He says that this won't be easy. It will be painful and slow and if you aren't a willing participant, all of my caring in the world won't matter.

"Furthermore, Roger stresses that you must deal with the past or go on suffering. I think you have to recognize that, right off the bat. You have to make yourself understand that we are trying to address the deaths of your parents, the crash itself, and your resulting phobias and sorrows."

CJ swallowed hard. Her face paled slightly. "You're asking quite a bit," she responded.

Brad's serious expression softened. "I know I am. It may sound stupid, but there's this image of the real Curtiss Jenny O'Sullivan that I see in my mind, and I'd very much like to get to know her. But only if you want it that way."

CJ took in Brad's words and sorted them into an acceptable form. "I want to know how you plan to do this. I want to know the details. That's another of my demands." Her words hit their mark, and now it was Brad's turn to swallow hard.

"I thought we'd start with some books. You can come over here or I can come to your place. I have a great many books on flying, air shows, and. . . ," he paused, "your father."

CJ steadied herself. "Go on."

"Well, I figured we could read about different flight-related activities, then graduate up to videos, and eventually pull in more personal items."

"Such as?" CJ questioned curiously.

"For starters, Cheryl tells me you have a storage unit filled with memorabilia. When you feel up to it, we could go through it. I also have some video tape that deals exclusively with your father's career and includes some family shots, as well."

CJ could only nod. It all seemed overwhelming. "I'd rather we meet here," she finally said. "My place seems too personal and I'm not sure I'm ready for that. And we both know your house at the airfield is out of the question."

"Meeting here is fine. But let's keep it as informal and friendly as possible. We are friends, after all. No set appointments. . .just get-togethers."

CJ smiled. "That does sound better."

æ

A couple of nights later, CJ sat beside Brad on the sofa.

"Did you have your people check out my financial status?" he asked, surprising CJ.

She nodded. "I did what you asked of me. Everything checked out, just like you said it would. My accountant, in fact, was very impressed. He kept going on and on about your portfolio. Maybe you two should spend some time together."

Brad chuckled at her teasing mood. How he wished she could maintain that lightheartedness throughout the evening ahead.

"Do you feel more comfortable about spending time with me? Are you convinced that I'm not after your money?"

CJ smiled. "My accountant assured me I could only benefit by spending time with you. I think he's hoping for trade secrets. Shall I play the spy?"

"Don't invest in hotels," Brad offered. "That's the best advice I can give."

Amusement lit up CJ's eyes. "Yes, I can see how you've suffered."

Brad rolled his eyes. "This is the longest I've stayed in one place. If it weren't for you, I'd probably be in Vail or Telluride."

"Do you have resorts there, as well?"

"Didn't you check that out?" Brad questioned.

"Umm. . . ," CJ tried to remember what her accountant had told her. "I guess I remember something about it. It wasn't all that important." She stopped abruptly and apologized. "I'm sorry. That didn't come out the way I meant it."

"It's all right, CJ. I don't offend easily. Is there anything you'd like to know about me that your accountant didn't find out?"

CJ leaned back against the plush couch and sighed. "Do you have brothers or sisters?"

"No."

"Do you have a college education?"

"Yes. I have two bachelor degrees. One in business administration, the other in hotel management. And I have a master's in public administration, as well."

"What? No doctorate?" CJ teased.

"Give me time. I'm only thirty," he said, feigning exasperation.

"Ah, now things are getting interesting. When is your birthday?"

"February 24," he replied. "Yours?"

CJ grinned. "I'm the one who's supposed to ask the questions."

Brad leaned back and folded his arms. "We're supposed to be friends. Can't friends know when each other was born?"

CJ took pity on him. "July 17."

"Been to college?"

"Yes." CJ couldn't help but grin at him. "Art history degree. Now there's something that will take you far."

Brad laughed. "Anything else?"

CJ sobered. "Are your parents still alive?"

Brad shook his head. "I lost them both when I was twenty-three."

"How?" she questioned softly.

"My father suffered a massive heart attack. He died instantly."

"What about your mother?" CJ forced herself to ask.

"I believe she died of a broken heart. She went downhill in a big way after Dad passed on. There was nothing I could do to comfort her. Within six months she was gone."

"I'm sorry, Brad." CJ's voice held tenderness and compassion.

"They're in heaven, and it's not the end," he said in a poignant way that CJ understood.

For several minutes, they sat in silence. Brad wanted CJ to have plenty of time to deal with the information, while CJ came face to face with another person's tragedies.

"Are you ready to look at some books?" Brad finally asked.

CJ nodded. "Maybe you could tell me what you have planned."

"I have a coffee table book, filled with beautiful photographs of airplanes. Some are in flight and some are on the ground. I thought for tonight, we could just look at the pictures and if you wanted to talk about anything, that'd be fine, too. If not, we'll just enjoy each other's company. Okay?"

CJ took a deep breath and looked at Brad. Enjoying his company wouldn't be hard. Keeping her emotions under control would be the major battle. "All right," she replied and forced herself to add, "let's get started."

eight

CJ found Brad's patience could very nearly disarm her concerns and fears. He was gentle with his questions and always eased up when he felt that probing into the past was becoming too difficult for her to handle.

She finally agreed to attend a Bible study with him and enjoyed the event in a way she'd not expected. The people gathered at the church were mostly singles, and before the study began, Roger Prescott led the group in a discussion of their concerns and problems for that week.

CJ listened in earnest interest as one person after another relayed the frustrations they had endured. Some spoke of loneliness or fears of being alone. Others mentioned difficulties at work or pressures to settle down and marry. One woman spoke of the lingering illness of her mother and how hard it was to watch her die, little by little, each day. For the first time, CJ could see merit in a quick and painless death such as her parents had shared.

When everyone had voiced something, with the exception of CJ and Brad, Roger led the group in prayer and asked God to surround each person individually with His protection and to bless them each in a special way. CJ felt the prayer go straight to her soul, and she clung to each word as though it were prayed for her alone.

"If everyone will open their Bible," Roger began, "we'll get started. Last week we moved into the second chapter of Ephesians. Does anyone recall something special about our study?"

One petite, dark-haired woman raised her hand. "I had never read this part of the Bible before and I guess I was pretty amazed by the clarification that Satan really is at work on earth. I guess I knew from things I'd been told that Satan was genuine, but the idea of him working in those around me was a concept I couldn't make real. That is, until we read that verse."

Roger nodded. "Let's all look again at the second chapter, verses one and two. I'll read out of the New International Version, so those of you who are following in another style, bear with me. 'As for you, you were dead in your transgressions and sins, in which you used to live when you followed the ways of this world and of the ruler of the kingdom of the air, the spirit who is now at work in those who are disobedient.' I guess we all recognize Satan in that passage. We can also see here that 'the ways of this world' are not God's ways. Anyone else have something they want to share?"

The man seated beside CJ spoke up. "I liked the fact that verse six says we've already been raised up with Christ."

"Good," Roger agreed. "Verse six says, 'And God raised us up with Christ and seated us with him in the heavenly realms in Christ Jesus.' We need to understand, folks, salvation began when we accepted Christ, and with salvation, eternity also begins for us as Christians. We don't need to keep waiting for our eternal blessings. We can take possession of them now!"

CJ tried to take it all in. Not only had it been a long time since she'd given any real attention to the Scriptures, but she'd never experienced this kind of Bible study in her life. Sunday sessions of church left a great deal unanswered, and it was easy to see why people were drawn to more in-depth readings of the Word. For CJ, it was like a feast of spiritual food, and she was nearly starved to death for it.

"If no one else wants to add anything, we'll start tonight's study with verse eight and read through to ten." Roger waited for everyone to find their place, then continued. " 'For it is by grace you have been saved, through faith—and this not from yourselves, it is the gift of God—not by works, so that no one can boast. For we are God's workmanship, created in Christ Jesus to do good works, which God prepared in advance for us to do.' Who would like to comment on this section of Scripture?"

"I'd like to say, 'Thank God!' " one man replied, and the group chuckled in unison before the man continued. "I'd be in a bad way if I had to get to heaven on my own."

"We all would be," Roger admitted. "Paul, the writer of this letter, above everyone else seemed to recognize this. He makes comments throughout his letters of how hard he tried to do the right thing, only to fail. If our salvation depended on whether or not we could tow the line and be perfect, as Christ is perfect, no one would make it into heaven. That's not to say we don't try to be as Christ."

CJ was stunned. It was as if Roger's words were aimed directly at her heart, yet this was a concern she'd shared with no one. Not even Cheryl or Brad.

Roger continued with CJ's eyes fixed intently upon him. "Let's break it down. We are saved by grace. What is grace?" Silence met the question and Roger did what he often did when this happened—he pulled out a dictionary.

"The closest definition I find here would be, 'Divine love and protection bestowed freely upon mankind. A virtue or gift granted by God.' We are saved by divine love and protection. We are saved through a gift God freely bestowed upon mankind. He didn't offer it with the expectation that we should pay something in return. He didn't offer it because of what we could do. He gave us salvation because

He loves us.

"Now, look further at that verse," Roger continued. " 'Through faith—and this not from yourselves, it is the gift of God.' We just established that, didn't we?" Several people murmured affirming words before Roger continued. "Now we've gone over this before, but who can tell me what faith is?"

The woman whose mother was dying raised her hand. "Hebrews 11:1 says, 'Now faith is being sure of what we hope for and certain of what we do not see.' Sometimes," she admitted, "that verse is all that gets me through."

"Exactly. Now, Paul knew there would be those do-gooders who would try to convince people otherwise. People who would proclaim that unless you performed sacrificial acts of worthiness and deeds of devoted worship, you would lose your salvation. He covers that neatly in verse nine when he says, 'not by works, so that no one can boast.'

"We can't work ourselves into heaven. However, God does expect us to live for Him, and in doing so, we find verse ten applies to how we are to go about it: 'For we are God's workmanship, created in Christ Jesus to do good works, which God prepared in advance for us to do.' "

CJ reread the words until she knew them by heart. "Not by works!" Her pulse quickened. She'd always believed that she had to be good, do good, in order to get to heaven and see her parents again. Now, she was hearing and reading that this wasn't the case. God expected her, as His child, to do good works which He had prepared for her, but not in order to earn her salvation.

The study continued, but CJ was lost in thought. She barely heard Roger announce that it was time to end in prayer. Everything seemed overwhelming.

❧

On the ride home, Brad chanced a question. "Tell me about your brother."

CJ flashed a bittersweet smile. "Curt is five years older than me. Even so, we were very close. He used to hang around with Cheryl and me and tease us unmercifully."

Brad said nothing. He recognized the fragile web that CJ spun.

"Whenever we were on a circuit of air shows and his college breaks coincided with a performance," CJ continued, "Curt would fly in and join us. Daddy always liked to have him along. . .said it made his job a whole lot easier. Our last performance was in Kansas. We finished up and had a really great meal of Chinese food with Cheryl and her dad. Curt had already gone back to college, and Cheryl was pining away for him." CJ glanced up suddenly. "I don't remember. . .did I tell you that Cheryl and my brother were engaged to be married?"

"No, but it sounds like you were all a close-knit family."

CJ nodded. "We were, until the accident. Now, in the five years that have past, I've managed to drive both Cheryl and Curt away."

"What makes you think you had that responsibility?" Brad pulled into the parking lot of CJ's apartment complex and shut off the engine.

"Curt left shortly after bringing me home to recuperate. I'm afraid I wasn't a good patient. I insisted he move me to a new house. I couldn't bear to be in the old one without my mom and dad. All the responsibilities of the funeral. . ." CJ felt her throat tighten. "I couldn't even go to my parents' funeral.

"My leg was shattered in the accident. Mangled might be a better word. I had to have fourteen separate pieces of debris surgically removed from my leg. Some were pieces of metal, others wood and fiberglass. The bone was broken in seven places, and the doctor wasn't even sure he could save it. Curt flew in a team of the best orthopedic surgeons in the country and wouldn't allow them to amputate. I had over three years of physical therapy, and I guess that only helped to make me more reclusive."

"What about Cheryl and Curt? Did they marry?"

"No. Curt changed after the accident. He tried to keep it inside, but I knew he was just as devastated as I was. When the press and the FAA came to my hospital room, Curt was most protective. Everything was so stressful. He and Cheryl started fighting. She couldn't understand why he'd shut her out. He couldn't deal with her constant clinging and questions. After Curt managed to get me and the estate settled, he took off—without a word—for three weeks."

"That must have frightened you a great deal," Brad declared.

"It was all of my worst nightmares come true. All I had left was Cheryl, and she grew distant and eventually began to travel with her jetset friends. She'd get so upset with me and say, 'You'll have to fly again sometime, CJ, why not just come along with me to Rio or Paris?' "

CJ paused and grew even more introspective. "It really wasn't Cheryl's fault, though. She also had to deal with her father. He and Daddy were best friends. They even invested in the air show business together and started their own aviation company. In fact, when Daddy put together a performance team, Ben Fairchild put together an impressive ground crew, just to see to our needs."

" 'Our needs'?" Brad questioned, sitting up and leaning forward. "Do you mean you were a part of the performance team?"

CJ smiled. "You couldn't be Doug O'Sullivan' s daughter

and not pilot a plane. I could handle a plane before I could ride a bicycle, even if I couldn't fly legally by myself. I'm still not all that good at riding a bicycle."

"And you performed in the air shows?" Brad was completely taken back.

"In whatever way I could. Daddy said a child behind the stick always brought in the crowd, and the crowd was everything to my father." CJ closed her eyes for a moment, and when she opened them again, tears streamed down her cheeks. "Missing them just isn't an adequate enough word."

Brad patted the seat beside him and CJ automatically scooted closer. CJ allowed Brad to encircle her with his arms. "No words can fill the void it leaves behind when we say good-bye to someone we love. Just remember, CJ," Brad whispered against her ear, "you've only said good-bye for a little while."

CJ said nothing. She let the tears fall in a quiet state of mourning while Brad rocked her gently in his arms. It was a slow release of pain and sorrow, and only the first in many steps that would be necessary to free herself from the accident.

&

Days later, CJ found herself thinking back to that moment in Brad's car. She hadn't gotten sick from reliving some of the past, and that, to her, was one of the very best signs. She began to feel better about herself almost immediately.

After donning cream-colored slacks and a burgundy silk blouse, CJ hurriedly attached gold dangling hearts to her ears and took a final look in the mirror. Hating the way her hair looked, CJ grabbed her brush, swept her hair back from one side, and secured it with a barrette. Deciding the results were acceptable, she repeated the action with the other side.

She was going to spend the day with Brad, and for some

reason, she felt like dressing up for him. She knew he'd stressed that they should be only friends but, in truth, part of her disliked the limitation. *Maybe he's not attracted to me*, CJ thought. *Maybe I should dress up more and really turn on the charm.*

She smiled to herself. It was the first time in her life she'd ever considered trying to attract a man's attention. She hadn't felt this good in years and, for once, CJ could actually say she felt hopeful.

Mrs. Davis had created another of her culinary delights. Sweet-and-sour meatballs were served on beds of steaming white rice, with stir-fried vegetables on the side. CJ couldn't remember when food had tasted so good.

After lunch, Brad led CJ into one of the side rooms, dominated by a big-screen television. A VCR sat conspicuously on the coffee table, and Brad motioned her to take a seat.

"I found something really special. I know I promised to tell you everything ahead of time, so I'm going to explain myself here and now," Brad began.

CJ looked warily around the room. Up until now, things had been going her way. She could only guess what Brad had planned. She watched suspiciously as he walked over to a handcrafted, oak sideboard and pulled open a drawer.

"I found a movie that had been made at one of the air shows when you were quite young. It's a very personal film, devoted to your family, especially your father. I had it transferred to video tape and thought we could watch it together. Are you game?"

CJ paled a bit and sat back hard. She hadn't even looked at photographs of her parents since the accident. "I don't know, Brad. I mean we've watched other videos and that went all right, but this is different."

"Look, I promise I'll turn it off if it gets to be too much. In fact, here." He reached over and handed her the remote control. "You're in charge."

CJ stared at the black-and-silver remote in her hand. She was in charge? Since when? She would have laughed out loud if it weren't for the serious expression on Brad's face.

Taking a deep breath, CJ decided to risk it. "Put the tape in."

The film started and for several minutes a narrator extolled the virtues of Douglas O'Sullivan in grand style. He told of her father's birth into a flying family. Her grandfather had barnstormed in his early days and later maintained one of the better flying circuses in America. Doug O'Sullivan was just as much a natural at flying as his father had been.

CJ smiled when they showed photographs of her father and grandparents. "They called him 'Scrappy' when he was a boy," CJ told Brad in a whisper. "On account of the fact he was so small."

The narrator spoke of other events in the life of Doug O'Sullivan. A distinguished career in the military, an honored war hero, and later, one of the forerunners in organizing international fly-ins, where people from all over the country could compete for prizes and laurels in flight performance. That brought the narrator to the place where he introduced the background.

CJ vaguely remembered the scene. It was one of the gatherings at Oshkosh, Wisconsin. Here was competition at its best. The camera panned the painted wooden banner. INTERNAT'L EXPERIMENTAL AIRCRAFT ASSOC., proudly labeled the top, and just beneath that, big, bold, yellow letters stated, FLY-IN CONVENTION. Flags from several nations, including the U.S., Canada, Britain, and France, graced the top of the banner and added an air of patriotic festivity to the day.

CJ was mesmerized as the tape rolled back the years. She

felt her stomach tighten as the camera zoomed in on a Curtiss Jenny biplane her father had called his baby. Usually, he flew the Jenny in ahead of the family while Curt and CJ's mother, Jan, would fly in later, bringing all the needed supplies for their stay.

"Nearly one million people will share the experience of this fly-in, and over fifteen thousand planes will take off and land on this runway before the week is out," the narrator was saying. The aerial view of the field was impressive, with row after row of planes anchored at the side of the airstrip.

"The numbers are staggering," the narrator continued. "They must find it quite a task to organize all of these aircraft."

"I'd imagine finding space to park the thirty or forty thousand campers that accompany folks here is more of a chore." CJ tensed and gripped the arm of the sofa. The voice belonged to her father.

The narrator continued. "Doug O'Sullivan, you've been flying most all of your life, isn't that true?"

"It sure is. Flying is my life," he was saying. CJ forced herself to look at the screen as the camera caught the tanned, leathery face of her father. "Of course," Doug O'Sullivan added, "I wouldn't have a life at all if it weren't for God. He's always been my co-pilot and always will be."

Tears blurred CJ's vision. *Oh, Daddy*, she thought, *why did you have to go away? Why did God take you from me?*

"You have quite a family, I understand," the narrator said. "I know folks would love to meet them."

"Well, over here is my oldest, Curtiss." CJ saw her dad put a possessive arm around Curt. "He's seventeen and handles the second biplane in our simulated dogfights. I'm sure you'll be able to catch us in the air later this afternoon."

Curt hammed for the camera and answered the questions directed at him before the men moved on to focus on Jan O'Sullivan, Doug's beloved wife. CJ felt her heart breaking. Her mother was radiant, youthful, and happy. She missed her so much, remembering their girl talks and the tenderness her mother had for her.

"There's not a gal around who can beat her. She's remembered by most for her multiple participations in the Powder Puff Derby," her father was saying of his wife. CJ watched her father lovingly pull her mother into his arms. "A pretty, young, talented woman is always good for the show, right?" Doug winked at the narrator, then planted a firm kiss on his wife's lips.

"Oh, Doug!" Jan exclaimed and feigned disgust. "You'll have to excuse him for his lack of manners," she laughed. "He's eaten and slept biplanes for so long, he doesn't know how to act in front of respectable people."

The film broke away to some previously recorded footage of her parents' earlier days as a team. The narrator told of the couple's harrowing experiences and triumphant successes. CJ wiped away the tears with her hand, then gratefully took a handkerchief Brad offered her.

"Last, but certainly not least," the reporter said, bringing the viewers back to Oshkosh, "is the youngest member of this flying team. I understand your daughter is only twelve, but already she flies like a pro."

"She certainly does. She's a great mechanic, too," Doug O'Sullivan said with pride. He was seated beside the narrator beneath a tent awning. "CJ!" he called. It was more than she could bear. CJ softly sobbed into the handkerchief, not even aware that Brad had slipped his arm around her.

A twelve-year-old CJ appeared on the screen. She was giggly and pigtailed and totally devoted to her father. She threw herself onto her father's lap in little-girl abandonment. Doug O'Sullivan tickled his daughter, until a laughing CJ yelled, "Oh, Daddy, stop!" Settling down, CJ faced the interviewer like she'd done it all her life.

"CJ O'Sullivan, I understand you have quite an interesting story behind your name," the narrator said.

"My daddy named me after his biplane," the little girl answered. CJ could barely hear the words. "I'm Curtiss Jenny O'Sullivan." Until that moment, CJ hadn't remembered even doing the interview. Now it all came flooding back to her.

"What a name and what a young lady!" the man replied.

"That she is," CJ heard her father say. "She's my special angel, and I love her very much."

CJ, the little girl on the screen, giggled and kissed her father. "I love you, too, Daddy." She laughed and danced away from the camera.

CJ, the woman, lifted the remote and murmured two words, "No more!"

nine

CJ broke down and cried with all her heart. Five years of pent-up loneliness and hurt came pouring out with the tears. Brad held her close, whispered comfortingly into her ear, and refused to let her bear the sorrow alone.

Little by little, instead of easing, CJ's pain intensified. Then came anger and resentment that CJ could no longer bury. Without warning, she pushed away from Brad and threw the remote control across the room. Her eyes caught the book on the end table, and she threw it, too.

Jumping up from the couch, CJ was like a wild, crazed animal, hurting and wounded so deeply that she refused to be consoled.

"He could have let them live!" she raged. "God didn't have to take them. I lived! They could have survived, as well. Why? Why did I have to be left behind? It isn't right! It isn't fair!"

By this time, Brad had gotten to his feet and closed the distance between them. "CJ, you've got to calm down."

"Stay away from me. Don't touch me," she managed to say between her clenched jaws. "I don't want to feel better. I don't want to be comforted. I can't bear the way you're looking at me now! I don't want your pity, and I don't want your sympathy."

Brad froze in midstep. "Is that what you think I want to give you? Pity? Sympathy? Grow up a little, CJ. Your temper tantrum at God won't change a thing. They're still dead."

CJ's mouth dropped open in surprise, but the tirade halted,

at least momentarily. Brad used the opportunity to continue.

"I care about you, CJ. I thought highly of your father, but he's beyond caring about my devotion. He's at peace with His Savior, and he would want you to be, as well." Brad walked toward her in slow, deliberate steps.

"I want to give you many things, CJ, but pity is not one of them. Pity cripples and kills, and I will not be part of it. I offer you friendship. Take it or leave it, but please don't spoil my heartfelt concern with your own self-pity." He stood directly in front of her. He could see the terror and rage in her eyes.

CJ drew a ragged breath. Everything Brad had said was right. "I don't want to be left behind," she whimpered. "I have nothing. Even my brother ran away to be rid of me. I'm alone, and it scares me."

Brad opened his arms, waiting for her move. CJ hesitated for only a moment, then threw herself into the welcoming embrace. "You're not alone anymore, CJ. I'm here, and I'll be here as long as you want me to be."

CJ said nothing. It was enough just to hear the declaration of faithfulness. She reveled in it. She embraced it. In that moment, she wanted nothing more than to feel the blanket of protection that Brad Aldersson offered her.

She lost track of how long they stood there, but finally Brad led her back to the couch and sat down with her.

"Being angry at God is probably the biggest guilt you've buried inside," Brad whispered. "You wanted so much to be good in order to earn your way into heaven, but deep down inside, you knew you harbored this horrible thing. You blame God for taking your parents. You blame God for your pain."

CJ nodded. He was right. How could he know so much about her? It was if she had laid her soul open for him to read, page by page.

"They're gone, and I'm here," she said hoarsely.

"But you aren't alone," Brad stressed.

"But I feel alone," CJ responded, looking deep into his eyes. She placed her hand over her heart. "I'm alone and lost inside, and I don't know how to find my way back."

Brad reached out and took her hand. Slowly, never taking his eyes from hers, he pulled her hand to his chest. "You're not alone," he repeated. "God never left you alone, CJ. You may have walked away, but He didn't. . .and neither will I."

༉

When CJ had finally calmed down enough to meet with Brad's approval, she made her way home and took a long, hot shower. Knowing she should call Cheryl but feeling unable to deal with her friend, CJ unplugged her phone and went to bed early.

For several hours, she stared at the ceiling. Her head was flooded with images from the past. In spite of how she tried to block their entry, the memories were there, and they forced her attention from every corner of her mind.

Tossing and turning, CJ struggled to find peace. It was clear that God was dealing with her, she realized, but what did He want? Absolution? He certainly didn't need forgiveness from her. After all, God hadn't held the grudge all these years, CJ had. God was innocent of the ugliness that bred contempt within her.

God was innocent!

The words hit her like a wall of stone. God had done nothing wrong. CJ was to blame for her own misery. She had allowed Satan a foothold, and now she was paying the price. Misery, paranoia, phobias, loneliness, anger—these were all things by which Satan could benefit. His purpose was served in these scornful attitudes; his and no one else's. CJ didn't have a life to call her own. She served those feelings as clearly as angels served their Lord in heaven.

No, she reasoned, *God doesn't need my forgiveness, but I need His.*

Yet, even knowing her need, CJ couldn't bring herself to ask for forgiveness. She felt the wall of protection going up around her. God, she rationalized, would understand just where she was coming from. God knew what pain she'd suffered and the battles she'd had to fight. And ultimately, CJ told herself, God had allowed everything that had happened to her. How could He still be a loving and merciful God and do that?

There was no peace for CJ that night. Nor in the nights that followed. She refused to plug her phone back in, and when Brad finally showed up at her door, she told him to go home.

CJ moved restlessly from room to room, never leaving the apartment for any reason. She wanted to make things right. She wanted to believe God was sovereign and righteous and loving, but her heart felt hardened with each day that passed and her mind told CJ she was justified to feel that way.

When finally she could bear no more of the alienation she'd created, CJ cried out to God, "I don't know what You want from me! You've already taken all that I loved. What more can I give?"

The resounding silence only made CJ feel worse. She paced a bit more, then settled down at her desk. Pushing up the roll-top cover, CJ's eyes caught sight of her Bible. She hadn't picked it up in days. Now, even though she fought the urge, CJ reached out and opened it.

Lamentations, a requiem of sorrow, greeted CJ's eyes, and she was drawn to the words that were spread out before her in the third chapter. "So I say, 'My splendor is gone and all that I had hoped from the Lord.' I remember my affliction and my wandering, the bitterness and the gall. I well remember them, and my soul is downcast within me. Yet this I call to mind and therefore I have hope: Because of the Lord's great love we are not consumed, for his compassions never fail. They are new every morning; great is your faithfulness."

Her eyes backed over the words, "I remember my affliction and my wandering, the bitterness and the gall." CJ not only remembered them, she wore them about her like a suit of armor that kept her from feeling or thinking or living.

CJ forced herself to concentrate on the last sentences: "Therefore I have hope: Because of the Lord's great love we are not consumed, for his compassions never fail." she stopped.

"But I feel like they've failed," CJ whispered. "I feel consumed." She read the last words: "They are new every morning, great is your faithfulness." CJ put her head upon the Bible and wept softly.

"I do want to believe that. I do want to trust You, God. I don't want this thing between us. Forgive me," she cried. "Just send me a sign. Show me what I must do in order to heal. I give up, God. I give up. There's nothing left."

It was almost startling the way peace began to infiltrate the rock-hard wall she'd placed around her heart. Slowly, CJ composed herself and got up. She'd wasted a great deal of time, not only during the last few days in her fight with God, but in her struggles against Him for over five years. What now? Recognizing the situation didn't make it disappear.

CJ wasn't surprised by the knock at her door, nor by the fact that it was Brad. Brad, however, was astonished at CJ's ragged appearance.

"Are you all right?" he questioned with a critical eye. Her eyes were puffy and swollen, with dark circles spoiling her perfect complexion.

"Yes and no." CJ pulled back from the doorway to add, "Want to talk about it?"

Brad smiled in a slight, almost impish way. "What do you think?"

CJ wearily stepped aside, letting Brad close the door behind him. She took herself to the couch and collapsed. Brad followed her in mute scrutiny. His face bore the concern that poured out from his heart.

CJ glanced up and almost laughed at his expression. "I look pretty bad, don't I?"

"Actually, you're a welcome sight. I was afraid I'd have to tear down that door. What have you been doing with yourself these past few days? You don't look like you've slept or eaten."

"I haven't," CJ admitted. "But I have been busy."

"Doing what?"

"Fighting." CJ's reply said it all.

"And who have you been fighting?" Brad questioned softly. The worried look faded into compassion.

"God. Myself."

"Who won?" Brad asked with a grin.

"Who do you suppose?" CJ countered with a laugh.

"Are you ready to try again?"

CJ pulled her knees up under her chin. She looked like a little girl, so vulnerable and lost. "I have to be," she answered. "I promised to go on."

"So now you're pulling yourself up by the bootstraps, is that it?"

CJ raised her head and shook it slowly. "I have no bootstraps," she replied. "All that is left in me is this weak, very tiny flicker of hope. Hope that God is really Who He says He is and that I can rest in that."

Brad reached out and squeezed her hand. "He's all that

He says and much, much more." Spying her Bible on the desk, he got up and walked over to retrieve it. "Lamentations?" he questioned, not really needing an answer.

CJ shrugged. "It's what I opened up to. I read from chapter three, through verse twenty-three."

Brad glanced down, then turned back to CJ with a smile. "You should have moved on down to the twenty-fifth and twenty-sixth verses."

"Well, don't just stand there," she replied. "Read it."

" 'The Lord is good to those whose hope is in him, to the one who seeks him; it is good to wait quietly for the salvation of the Lord.' " Brad closed the Bible, put it on the coffee table, and smiled. "That tiny flicker of hope is all you need, CJ. God will do the rest."

"I asked Him to show me what to do," CJ shared. "I asked for a sign."

"Come with me, then," Brad whispered. "Come see my biplanes."

CJ looked apprehensive. "You haven't forgotten how I reacted the last time, have you?"

"I haven't forgotten."

"Are you sure?"

Brad reached down and pulled her to her feet. "CJ, come see my planes. Let go of your fear and bank on that hope. God won't let you down."

"Because of the Lord's great love, we are not consumed," CJ murmured.

"What?"

"Nothing," CJ said, losing herself in his warm, green eyes. "Let's go see your planes."

ten

Moving down the interstate, CJ felt her apprehension grow. Could she really do this? Now that they were nearing the airstrip, she silently questioned the sensibility of the trip.

"Penny for your thoughts," Brad whispered.

"A penny's worth would take an hour," she replied, paying close attention to their approach to the airfield. She tried not to grimace, but Brad saw her expression before she carefully concealed it.

"If you don't feel up to getting out of the Jeep, we can just sit and talk."

CJ said nothing. She forced her gaze across the field to where someone was shooting touch and goes in a Piper Cub. Watching the plane land, circle the field, and take off again brought back memories of when her father had taught her to fly. Touch and goes were an important part of the routine in order to teach technique and hone skills for landings and takeoffs. She'd spent hours at the controls, with her father's gentle instructions helping her to correct each mistake.

Brad parked the Jeep and turned to face CJ. "Are you all right?"

She took a deep breath. Trepidation was a companion she knew well. Glancing back at the runway, she swallowed hard. "I think so," she finally replied.

"I meant what I said. I don't want you to force yourself. There's no sense in passing out again."

CJ tried to be lighthearted. "You're just afraid you'll have to carry me back to the car." Her blue eyes met his amused stare.

"That would be my pleasure," he said with a grin. "I couldn't possibly pass up the chance to get that close to you."

CJ lost herself for a moment. His eyes twinkled in a dazzling display that made her feel like laughing. The tiny crow's feet that edged them only made his smile more pronounced. Her heart quickened and pounded in a way she'd never noticed before. Fearing the truth, she told herself it was from apprehension and anxiety. But part of her wasn't convinced. Was she losing her heart to this man?

"Are you ready?" he asked and reached his hand out to cover hers.

CJ entwined her fingers with his and squeezed them tightly. "I'm so afraid," she whispered. "Inside the car it doesn't seem so bad, but out there. . ." She lifted her chin. "Out there, it's real and it's frightening."

"I'll stay right by your side. I'll even hold your hand. You won't be alone. God and I will be with you."

CJ searched Brad's face to confirm his declaration. Finding the affirmation she needed to see, CJ took another deep breath. "I'm ready."

Brad opened the door for her and pulled her close. "How's this?" he asked. CJ looked up, offered him a weak smile, but said nothing. They walked out toward the hangar, and Brad began to speak. "Any time you want to go back to the car, just tell me."

CJ nodded. Her head was already filled with the sights, sounds, and smells of the private airport.

"I bought extra property here so that I could keep all my planes in one place," Brad informed her. "I have six altogether. The four biplanes I want to show you are on the front side, over here." He pulled her along with him to an ultramodern, prefab metal hangar.

Dropping his arm for a moment, Brad fished out a set of keys and unlocked the building. Sweeping aside the doors, CJ gasped in surprise. The dimly lit interior of the hangar stood in sharp contrast to the contemporary exterior.

Brad flipped on the lights and drew CJ to his side. She let her eyes travel over the individual stalls where some of history's finest aviation wonders were housed. Memories rushed back in waves that threatened to drown her in sorrow.

Not even realizing it, CJ reached across and grabbed Brad's hand. Her breath caught in her throat.

"I'm sure you recognize them," Brad said softly against her ear. Indeed she did. They were some of her father's favorites.

"It's been a long time," CJ whispered, feeling the years fall away.

They walked by each plane, giving a cursory evaluation. The blue and white Waco with its enclosed cockpit and passenger cabin was similar to one that CJ's father had bought shortly before the accident. The red and white Travel Air, product of the business marriage between Cessna, Stearman, and Beech in 1924, waited regally. The model had always been one of CJ's favorites. Putting aside the horrors of her past, she reached out and touched the eight-foot prop.

"It's just like Daddy's," she murmured.

"I know. It was one of the first I purchased. Reading your father's first book, I fell in love with his description. He talked about how big and cumbersome most pilots thought the Travel Air was, but he didn't feel that way."

"That's true," CJ joined in, forgetting to be upset. "Daddy said it was all a matter of perspective. He loved the way it handled, and when I was with him in the Travel Air, I thought it was the most glorious plane in the world."

Brad smiled, knowing that for a brief moment, CJ was twelve years old again, with the wind in her hair and Doug

O'Sullivan at the stick.

"Over here's the old standard," Brad said, moving her on before she became morose.

"A Stearman," she said with a grin. "Daddy said you could fly them standing on your head."

"From the looks of some of the air show films, I'd say he did that once or twice," Brad laughed.

CJ found the experience much better than she'd thought it would be. All the years of worry were far more oppressive than the actual deed of standing there before the planes her father loved.

"And last, but not least," Brad said, "is this beauty. She's my favorite."

CJ stood before the de Havilland Tiger Moth. "Oh, Brad!" she exclaimed. "I can see why. What a beautiful plane!"

The plane had been restored to perfection, and CJ admired the hard work that had resulted in the masterpiece before her. "Dope and fabric never looked so good," she complimented.

"It took a lot of hours, but I enjoyed it all," Brad admitted. "Here, look at this," he said and led CJ to the place where a photograph was pinned up on the wall. "This is how she came to me."

"Now I'm really impressed," CJ said, looking at the photo. The plane in the picture barely resembled the majestic wonder that graced the hangar.

"They brought her in on the back of a truck. She couldn't even fly."

"Kind of like me," she murmured absent-mindedly.

CJ looked away from the picture to find Brad's face only inches from her own. She wondered for the briefest second if he would kiss her, and then the moment passed, unfulfilled.

Brad stepped away with a look of discomfort, and CJ wondered if she'd somehow done something wrong. She tensed up, feeling the tightness in her chest for the first time since entering the hangar. She put her hand to her throat, taking a deep breath.

Brad didn't notice the look on her face, as he moved back toward the Waco. "This is my newest in the collection," he said as though nothing had happened.

CJ moved to the Waco, working hard to keep her emotions under control.

"I've had to make some adjustments and repairs," Brad said, sounding very casual. "I put in a new engine, but I'm still having trouble with. . ."

Brad's words faded into CJ's imagination and took on the voice of her father. For a moment she was a little girl again, working alongside him, seeing the engines through his eyes, and touching them with his hands.

Without thinking, CJ voiced several suggestions for the problem at hand, and before Brad could answer, she continued, "I remember once when you were working on. . ." Her words fell into silence, as her eyes refocused on the hangar. CJ's head began to swim. The old feelings of weakness were making her legs rubbery.

"Brad," she whispered weakly.

He turned with a look of questioning, but quickly saw the problem. "Come on, let's get out here," he suggested.

CJ nodded. "I'm sorry. I don't know why—"

"Shhh," Brad interrupted, putting his finger to her lips. "We both knew this wouldn't be easy. I'm proud of you for even trying. Most folks wouldn't."

Once they were outside, CJ felt a little better. The Piper was no longer shooting touch and goes, and for the most part everything was quiet. For the first time, CJ realized it was a weekday, and she turned to Brad.

"Don't you ever work?" she asked.

Brad laughed. "Actually, it's funny that you should ask. I am planning on being out of town the rest of the week. I have to fly over to Telluride and see to some matters at the resort there. Want to come?"

CJ shook her head. "I'm not ready for that." She paused reflectively. "But ask me again, later."

"Don't worry, I will. Until then, what would you suggest we do next?"

CJ wanted to say something about their encounter in the hangar when she thought he might kiss her, but instead she shrugged and turned away.

"Did you have something in mind?" she asked, refusing to look at him.

"The Waco still needs work. How about coming out here on the weekends and helping me?"

CJ wondered how it would feel to work on planes again. She'd spent many hours with her father, tightening cylinder-base nuts, patching tears, replacing broken struts. She doubted there was a single part of any one of those planes that she hadn't worked on, in another time.

Summoning up her courage, CJ replied, "I suppose it would be a logical way to proceed. Also," she added, only now making up her mind, "I'm going to call Roger. I think I'm ready to talk with him."

Brad surprised them both by pulling CJ into his arms. He hugged her briefly, then set her away as though just realizing what he'd done. "That's fantastic news, CJ. I know you won't regret it."

"I'm sure I won't," CJ replied. "What I regret are the wasted years in between."

❧

More problems awaited CJ when she returned to her apartment. The telephone answering machine had a message on it from Cheryl. *Poor Cheryl,* CJ thought. *I really need to make up some time with her.*

Picking up the phone, CJ dialed her friend's hotel room.

"Hello," Cheryl answered without her usual enthusiasm.

"Cheryl? It's CJ."

"CJ! Are you all right? Where have you been? I've tried and tried to call. I couldn't even locate Brad to ask him whether he knew where you were."

"I'm really sorry," CJ apologized. "I've been working through the past, as you well know, and the other day, things just got to be too much. I'm better now, and I'm really sorry to have neglected you."

"As long as you're okay," Cheryl replied.

"So the big day is just a week away, eh?" CJ asked and got comfortable on the couch.

Cheryl didn't reply, and the silence from the other end of the line caused CJ to realize something was wrong.

"Cheryl?"

"There is no wedding. At least not for a while," she finally answered. "Stratton and I had a fight and he walked out. He called me several days later and asked me to postpone things until he could clear his head."

"Sounds like he has a hole in it if he's letting you get away," CJ countered.

"I just feel so. . ."

"Disappointed?" CJ suggested.

"Yeah, and lonely," Cheryl replied.

"Say, I have an idea," CJ began. "Why don't you move in with me for a while. It would take care of the lonely part, anyway."

Cheryl didn't say anything for a moment, but then with a childlike voice, she questioned, "When?"

CJ laughed. "Today. Right now. As soon as we hang up, just load up and come ahead. I'll be here."

"Are you sure a certain hotel owner wouldn't be a bit miffed? After all, he won't have you all to himself anymore."

"Brad and I are just good friends," CJ said sternly.

"Yeah, sure."

"Cheryl, are you trying to get me to change my mind?" CJ didn't wait for an answer. "I'll expect you by five. Now get packing."

CJ hung up the phone, but Cheryl's call had caused her to think. For the first time she realized that her feelings for Brad were quite strong. She depended on their friendship in a way she'd never depended on anyone before. The phone rang again, breaking her concentration.

"Hello?"

"Hi, it's Brad. I just wanted to tell you good-bye. I've got the plane packed, and I'll be taking off for Telluride today instead of tomorrow."

CJ felt a lump in her throat. "It'll be dangerous, flying over the mountains and all. I remember all about wind sheers and downdrafts. Stay away from the ridges," she instructed.

Brad laughed. "Yes, Mother."

CJ tried to be as amused, but she was startled at the feelings that surfaced inside her. "Sorry," she finally said.

"Don't be. I like your being concerned for me. Take care, and I'll see you Saturday."

"Brad!" She said his name in near panic. Had he already hung up?

"Yeah?" His voice calmed her nerves.

"Please be careful."

"Stop fretting, CJ. I've got a twin-engine Beech, and she's a real honey of plane. . .plenty of power and I've had her for some time. It's going to be all right. I'll call you tonight, okay?"

"Okay, bye."

CJ hung up the phone feeling strangely calm. Brad was a good pilot, and he could handle himself just fine. Of course a few prayers couldn't hurt, CJ thought, and immediately offered one up for his safety.

eleven

Summer waned, moving into autumn with a golden glow of quaking aspen. The mountainsides turned colorful in shades of red, orange, and yellow, as the season placed its mark on the land. Amid this change, CJ found her Saturdays consumed with the sights and sounds of Brad's private hangar. She relished their time together, realizing that for the first time since the accident she actually felt happy.

On three different occasions, when they labored for several hours in the hangar, Brad suggested they move up to his house for refreshment and a rest, but CJ refused. In spite of her security with Brad, she felt the house signaled something too personal. It was one thing to go to his office/apartment at the hotel penthouse, but for some reason the three-story, native-stone residence made CJ uneasy.

Brad didn't seem to mind, but CJ still felt she owed him an explanation. One day, after several hours of silent work over the Travel Air, CJ found the words.

"I feel like I should explain to you about the house," CJ began. "I guess it sounds crazy, but it's just too much for me," she said softly and added, "at least, right now."

Brad smiled and reached out with a rag to wipe grease from her chin. "I wasn't offended. I figure when the time is right, you won't be uncomfortable. When it's important to you, you'll show up under your own steam, and I probably won't even have to extend the invitation."

Brad quickly moved on to another subject, and CJ breathed a sigh of relief.

The situation with the house did bother Brad, but what could he say? Days passed and he contemplated CJ's fears with a deep, dreaded kind of concern. Maybe she was put off by him. Maybe she was just seeking to keep things from becoming too familiar. . .too personal.

That night, to his surprise, CJ telephoned. It was the first time she'd ever called him directly at home.

"This is a treat," he said, recognizing her voice.

"I thought it about time," CJ admitted.

"Indeed," he replied. "I suppose I can expect a visit to the house to be not far behind."

"Don't rush me," CJ answered in a light manner. "You, above everyone, should know I work at my own pace."

"Speaking of paces, I've been thinking about something, and I wanted to talk to you about it."

"Sounds ominous," CJ said in a hesitant voice. "I'm not sure I want to hear it."

"Well, just listen and don't interrupt," Brad said sternly. "I think it's time you tried to fly again. I don't expect you to pilot or anything like that. Just a simple buzz around the field. I wouldn't make you stay up very long, and you could call it quits when you'd had enough."

There was dead silence on the other end of the phone. Brad's forehead furrowed in frustrated worry, anticipating her response. Finally, CJ spoke.

"I don't know."

Brad felt elated. She hadn't said no. "Well," he said, "maybe you could just think it over and we'll pray about it, too."

"All right."

"Thatta girl!" he exclaimed.

&

When Saturday arrived, CJ drove up to the airfield and parked beside Brad's hangar. She got out of the car and stared back at the house for several minutes. It was a beautiful home, she thought. Three floors of sandy brown, native-stone, with balconies on the second and third levels. Beamed cathedral ceilings could be seen in the lower level through full-story, arched windows. CJ thought it a masterpiece of architecture.

Turning away, she moved to the hangar. Finding the doors already pushed back, CJ entered, fully expecting to find Brad already at work.

"I'm here," she called. Silence met her declaration, and CJ frowned slightly. "Brad?"

Nothing. CJ reasoned that he must have gone up to the house for some reason and she decided to wait until he returned. She moved from plane to plane, feeling on an intimate level with each one. No one could spend the hours she had working on these planes' bodies and engines without feeling a special kinship with them.

Reaching the Travel Air, CJ put her hand out and ran it along the back portion of the fuselage. It was sleek with its multiple coats of hand-rubbed butyrate dope and paint. CJ moved up to the wing, and before she gave herself time to think, she stepped up onto it and propelled herself into the cockpit.

For a minute, she did absolutely nothing. Sitting in the silence, CJ squeezed her eyes closed tightly and concentrated on the feel of the cockpit. It felt like the arms of an old friend encircling her as she sat there, yet she still felt uncomfortable. Without opening her eyes, CJ reached forward and felt the stick, the instrument panel—old memories blended with new feelings. It was all coming back.

Brad had heard the car pull in and finished with the phone call that had taken him from the hangar. He stood in the entryway to the building, afraid to say a word as he focused on CJ's coppery head peaking out from the cockpit of the Travel Air.

He didn't know if she'd heard him enter or felt his presence, but CJ opened her eyes and met his as he waited there for her. She pushed back her hair and stood to get up. Brad quickly came to the plane and helped her down from the wing.

It was one of those moments that both Brad and CJ realized had been intended for something more than words. Brad wrapped her in his arms and swung her out away from the plane and then refused to let her go. Feeling her melt against him, Brad nearly moaned aloud. Instead, he pulled back slowly, knowing that he was about to cross the barrier line he'd put in place between them. CJ turned her face upward as if the whole thing were choreographed by someone else. Brad lowered his lips to hers, hesitating only a brief second before they touched and sealed the moment. The line had been crossed!

"I'm so proud of you," Brad whispered. "You've worked so hard to put your fears to rest. I know your folks are smiling down from heaven. You've almost made it, CJ."

"I couldn't have done it without you," she admitted and stepped away. "You've taught me a great deal these past months, and I'm grateful."

Brad thought he noted hesitation in her voice and hurried to ask, "So do we fly today?"

She looked from the plane to Brad and then turned away. "I don't think I can."

Brad came up behind her and pulled her back against him. He just held her.

"I know you're afraid," he finally whispered. "I can wait for you to deal with it. But I have a suggestion that might help."

CJ took a deep breath. "What is it?"

"Why don't we just taxi out and back. We won't even leave the ground, and you can just get used to the sound and feel of the plane again."

"That doesn't sound so bad," she replied. Then a look of doubt crossed her face. "But what would keep you from taking off, anyway?" She turned and stepped back. "I couldn't stop you if you decided to force the situation."

Brad frowned. "You don't trust me? Have I ever done anything that would prove to you that I'm other than a man of my word?"

She put out her hand, intending to do nothing more than touch his shoulder. Instead she allowed her fingers to reach up and trace the tense line of his jaw.

"Can we take the Travel Air?" she asked in a voice that reminded Brad of a little girl.

He took hold of her fingers and kissed them before letting go. A smile replaced the frown, revealing that all was forgiven. "We'll take whichever one you like."

CJ smiled. "Do you have any airsickness bags?"

Brad threw back his head and laughed. "I don't think so, but we'll find something suitable if it means the difference between your scratching the mission and going through with it."

CJ shook her head, still smiling. "I just didn't want to make a scene. I figure I can pass out, and being strapped into the plane, I won't cause much of problem. But since I have to work on these things, I didn't want to have a mess to clean up."

"You won't get sick," he stated firmly.

"I won't get sick," she repeated, feeling a bit of confidence in the declaration.

"Come on," he said and held out his hand. "You'll see."

They taxied to the end of the runway with CJ tightly gripping the seat, eyes closed. She clenched her jaws together, until her gums ached in protest. Her stomach tightened, but only for a moment. Then Brad gave the engine a little power and CJ realized it was a pleasant sound, not a painful one.

The wind rushed up to meet her face, and CJ was grateful for the goggles that held her hair down against her head. She opened her eyes and realized that all was well. Relaxing against the bouncing motion as they moved back toward the hangar, CJ felt she'd once again met and conquered an important hurdle.

"Thank You, God," she breathed against the wind. "Thank You for helping me and thank You for Brad's patience with me."

twelve

In the days that followed, CJ gave heavy consideration to Brad's suggestion that she fly with him. She weighed the situation carefully, concluding that sooner or later she would have to face this final leg of recovery or forget about it all together.

This isn't going to get any easier, she told herself. *You've put things off for too long, as it is.*

It was very early, and having no idea whether Brad would be home or at the penthouse, CJ drove out to the airfield. She parked beside the hangar and, noting that Brad's Jeep was in its usual spot, bolstered her conviction with prayer.

"Father," she began, "I feel this is the direction You are leading me, but if it's not. . .if somehow I have misunderstood. . .please, let Brad be too busy to fly today. Amen."

With slow, determined steps, CJ walked up the cobblestone walkway to the front of the house. For a moment she stood before the arched, double doors, hesitating in her mission. She reached out her hand, took a deep breath, and pressed the button to ring the doorbell.

Silently, she counted to ten to keep her mind from insisting that she bolt and run. She'd just reached six when a rather disheveled Brad opened the door. For a moment he just stared in stunned disbelief, and then his look changed to amusement as he ran his hand back through his uncombed hair.

"You would show up today," Brad said with a chuckle. He quickly tucked in the tails of his long-sleeved shirt.

CJ wrinkled her nose, shrugged her shoulders, and turned

to go. Brad quickly reached out and turned her back around.

"Oh no, you don't. You aren't going anywhere. You think I don't know why you're here today, but I do."

CJ raised a questioning eyebrow. "Oh really?"

Brad pulled her toward the door. "You wouldn't have come to the house if it weren't very important, and I can only think of one very important issue that you would bring to me," he said, pulling her into the stylish entryway and closing the door behind her. "Now you can't run away," he grinned.

CJ leaned back against the door and smiled. "Well, if you can really read my mind, you'd know I have no intention of running away."

"I was just getting ready for the day. Why don't you come in and have some coffee while I finish?"

CJ glanced around to take in the small vestibule. "I suppose I could," she replied slowly. "But only if it won't take too long. I'm on a mission, you know."

"Yes, I know." His words were very nearly serious, and CJ didn't want the atmosphere to change from the light-hearted banter that she was enjoying.

"Do you make decent coffee?" she questioned.

Brad smiled, sensing her mood, and took hold of her arm. "Why, Miss O'Sullivan, I make the best coffee in the world. It's a very special blend that keeps busy pilots awake and on their toes."

CJ tucked her arm around his and allowed him to guide her to the kitchen. She noticed that the breakfast bar was covered with papers and a small notebook computer. "If I'm keeping you from working, I can come back," she offered.

Brad tightened his hold. "You know better. Now, sit here." He directed her to a stool and moved the papers aside. Bringing the pot and a mug bearing his hotel logo, Brad poured a cup of coffee and handed it to CJ.

"So you take cups from hotels?" she mused, examining the mug. "Most people go for the towels or an occasional highboy."

Brad laughed. "I know the owner and he doesn't mind at all."

"He does seem to be an awfully patient sort," CJ agreed, taking a long sip of the hot liquid. She put the cup down and met Brad's amused stare. "And very considerate," she added.

"Sounds like you're kind of fond of this guy," Brad teased. "I might have competition."

CJ feigned shock. "Well he certainly isn't as brash and forward as you, but alas," she paused and took another drink, "I'm certain he can't make coffee anywhere near this good." She batted her eyes, enjoying the game.

"You like it, then?"

"What?" CJ asked innocently. "The coffee or the maker?"

"You have my permission to elaborate on both," Brad said and leaned back against the butcher block that dominated the center of the room.

"I thought you had something to do," CJ said. "Looks to me like you could use a shave."

Brad grinned broadly. "Looking out for your own interests, I see."

Confusion registered on CJ's face, confirming that she didn't catch his meaning. Brad walked to where she sat, leaned down, and kissed her cheek, making certain that his whiskery chin rubbed against it lightly.

"I see what you mean," she said and blushed deeply. She hadn't expected the kiss or the suggestive teasing.

Brad reached out and touched his fingers to her coppery curls, letting one wrap around his finger. "I'll go shave and then we'll discuss where you want to fly to."

CJ sat waiting for Brad to return, still contemplating his words. He seemed to know automatically that she was here to fly. How could he know her so well?

She drained the cup of coffee and felt a little less nervous as she allowed her gaze to travel around the room. Copper-bottomed pots and pans hung over the butcher block in the center of the room, with a multitude of spices and condiments lining the middle of the broad workstation.

The room was light and airy. CJ thought it very much what she would like for her own, if she ever bought a house.

"I told you I wouldn't be long," Brad said minutes later. He reappeared, pulling on a navy blue sweater.

CJ blushed, noting that he had shaved. She lowered her head, pretending to concentrate on the empty cup, hoping that Brad hadn't seen her embarrassment.

She thought she'd pulled it off until he joined her at the table with the pot and his own cup. "You look very charming when you blush. More coffee?"

CJ started to laugh, although she wasn't really sure why. It suddenly all seemed so funny. There she sat, trying so hard to be professional and disengaged from her emotions while they screamed to be recognized from every portion of her being. There was no sense in trying to conceal her feelings from Brad. He always seemed to know exactly what she was thinking and feeling.

Brad didn't say a word. He poured them both more to drink, then sat down beside CJ at the table. He enjoyed her laughter and even more so, her embarrassment, for it spoke loudly of what CJ wouldn't say with words. He knew she cared for him, but he wanted quite badly to know how much. Breaking all of Roger's rules, Brad lost his heart completely when CJ lifted her ice blue eyes to meet his. She was everything to him, and Brad could no longer ignore his feelings for her.

"So you've decided to fly," he stated, refusing to drop his gaze.

"I, uh. . . ," she stammered. "Yes."

Brad nodded. "And where would you like to go, and which plane shall we take?"

CJ shook her head. "I don't want to go anywhere, and I'd just as soon we take the Travel Air."

Brad laughed and the spell was broken. "You don't want to go anywhere, but you want to get there in the Travel Air?"

"I just thought maybe we could shoot touch and goes or just circle the field. I don't want to get so far that I can't get back down. I don't want to move too fast and mess everything up."

Brad wondered if her words had a double meaning. "Okay," he answered. "We'll just circle and land. If you want more, we'll go again."

&

Moments later, CJ found herself in the cockpit of the Travel Air. "Are you ready?" Brad yelled above the plane's roar.

CJ couldn't really hear him, but she knew he was waiting for her okay. Without looking back, CJ waved her arms forward, knowing that Brad would understand. He did.

The plane moved forward as it had the time before when they'd taxied out and back. CJ forced herself to keep her eyes open. Reaching up, she adjusted the goggles and wondered what it would feel like to rush down the runway and feel the plane lift up into the air.

Because the Travel Air was a tail dragger, the nose of the plane was elevated and obstructed CJ's view down the runway. Nevertheless, she glanced out to the side and past the struts. Biplanes looked so frail compared to the modern mono-wing plane. Especially when you sized them up against the commercial planes, with their metallic glow and powerful jet engines. In reality, however, the biplane was a very reliable ship, and CJ took comfort in that fact as Brad revved up the engine.

In the next minute, they were rushing down the runway in a burst of energy. Autumn gave the wind a bite as it slammed against CJ's face. Twenty feet rolled by, then one hundred, then two hundred. CJ lost track and braced herself as she felt the familiar sensation of the plane lifting up from the ground.

In a flash of memory, she was a little girl again—five, maybe six years old. She felt the buckles that held her snug against the cockpit. "Whatever you do, Jenny," she could hear her father say, "don't unbuckle these."

As the plane climbed higher, Brad leveled the nose a bit. CJ looked down across the valley and held her breath. *Dear God,* she thought, *I'm really here and You are, too.* God was still God, and CJ sighed in relief.

Brad circled the airfield in a wide sweep. The plane moved through the skies with the grace and elegance of a refined old woman.

"Planes fly through the air, not over the ground, Jenny darlin'," her father would say, feigning an Irish brogue. He'd taught her important properties of flight from her earliest years. Bernoulli's theory was pounded in, explaining the way an airplane achieved lift as the air moved over the wing.

"Remember, Jenny, airplanes don't stall at a speed, they stall at an angle," he would say. It came back to her as though it'd been just yesterday.

Lost in thought, CJ panicked when the plane began to descend. She tried to throw herself forward, anticipating a crash. The harness held her fast and made her realize that all was well. Brad was simply landing the plane.

Brad was a gifted pilot and he touched the Travel Air down as though kissing the earth with the landing gear. They were level for several feet until the tail snapped down and the plane rolled to a stop at the end of the runway.

CJ felt like shouting. She'd done it! She'd actually flown, and she hadn't gotten sick or frightened. Well, not much, anyway.

Brad taxied back to his hangar and jumped from his seat as the propeller slowed and then stopped. He was at CJ's side instantly.

"You okay?"

CJ undid her harness and nearly leaped into his arms. "I did it, Brad! I really did it!" The enthusiastic smile on her face told him everything he needed to know.

He lifted her out of the cockpit and helped her off the wing. When they were both on the ground, he pulled her into his arms and whirled her around and around.

"I did it. I flew again!" she exclaimed over and over.

"You sure did!" Brad's enthusiasm matched her own.

When he stopped turning her around and her feet touched the ground once again, CJ lifted her face to his and waited for the inevitable to happen. She knew he would kiss her. She wanted him to. And then he did.

Taking her face in both hands, Brad looked at her lovingly for several heartbeats. His green eyes were dancing with laughter, but they were also bright with passion.

"I love you, CJ," he whispered, then lowered his lips to hers.

CJ's mind exploded in a riot of emotions and thoughts. *He loves me?* Had she heard him correctly?

The kiss deepened as if in answer, and CJ found her fears and concerns melting away. She wrapped her arms around his neck and, for the first time in her life, kissed a man in return.

When Brad pulled away, CJ kept her eyes closed and sailed away on wings all her own.

"CJ, did you hear me?"

"Ummm?"

"I said, I love you."

CJ's eyes snapped open. "Of course I heard you."

Brad laughed nervously. "I really do," he said, sobering slightly. "And not just because you got in that plane today and not simply because of all the hard work you did to defeat the ghosts of your past."

"No?" she questioned, needing and wanting to hear more.

"No. I love you for so many more reasons, and I can't even begin to tell you all of them."

"You could try," CJ said, dancing away with a teasing smile. "You could try." She picked up speed, threw a glance over her shoulder, and gave Brad a departing wink.

She ran out across the fading lawn and past the hangar, but by that time, Brad had caught up with her, grabbed her around the waist, and pulled her to him in a giant embrace. CJ laughed as she hadn't laughed since before the accident. She was happy and, for the first time in her life, she felt secure and free.

"I love your laugh. I love your hair when the sunlight hits it and makes it sparkle. I love the way your eyes light up when you're happy and the way you blush when you're embarrassed," Brad said, pulling away from her to look intently into her eyes.

Some of CJ's braid had pulled loose and several copper ringlets framed her face. A chill wind blew down from the Rockies, causing her to shiver.

"Come on," Brad said, putting his arm around her shoulders and steering her toward his home. "I'll make some more pilot coffee."

CJ thought he sounded strangely disappointed. Perhaps he had hoped that she'd return his declaration of love. Gently, she reached out to halt him. "Brad," she said softly, "thank you for taking me up and," she lowered her head and blushed, "for loving me."

Brad gave her shoulder a squeeze and walked on toward the house. "Getting you in the plane was real work, but loving you wasn't hard at all," he whispered and added a wink when CJ raised her face to his.

"Well, so much for just being friends," CJ laughed.

"Roger will no doubt chastise me for my lack of discipline," Brad replied, feigning sternness. "Good thing I didn't become a psychologist, eh?"

"I think you would have been great at helping people," CJ countered, enjoying the lazy walk back to the house.

"But then, I might have fallen in love with someone else," Brad said flatly.

They stopped walking and CJ felt her heart skip a beat. She warmed under the look he gave her and she felt her breath catch in her throat. "I don't think I would have cared for that," she managed to say.

"No?"

"No." The firmness of her reply was all the hope she would give him.

Unable to resist the windblown woman with glacier blue eyes, Brad encircled her waist with his hands and kissed her briefly once again.

"Can we do this every weekend?" CJ murmured as he pulled away.

Brad's laughter filled the air. "Kiss or fly?"

"Both," CJ responded boldly. "I think I need to get used to both."

It was late evening when CJ finally returned to her apartment. She'd enjoyed spending the entire day with Brad and felt only marginally guilty when she returned to find Cheryl somewhat concerned about her long absence.

"I had the most glorious day," CJ told her friend. "I flew, Cheryl. I flew in the Travel Air, and it was wonderful."

Tears filled Cheryl's eyes. She knew what this had cost CJ and how hard the choice had been.

"Oh, CJ," she said, embracing her friend, "I'm so happy. It's like a totally new start for you."

"The flight was only part of what made the day glorious," CJ admitted.

Cheryl stepped back with a questioning look. "Well?"

CJ laughed and pushed past her friend and down the hall. She stood outside her bedroom door and looked back at the puzzled Cheryl.

"He told me he loves me, Cheryl." Her giggles sounded like a child at play. "Brad loves me."

thirteen

Brad turned out the lights and made his way upstairs. His mind was filled with the image of copper curls, blue eyes, and warm, responsive lips. CJ!

He turned down the covers of his bed, grabbed his briefcase, and settled down to read quarterly reports from his resorts. He scanned the papers, noting with interest that additional land adjoining his Jackson Hole, Wyoming, property had come up for sale. The manager had been good enough to let him know before the property had been placed on the open market. It would make a great piece for a golf course or recreation center. He'd fly up there tomorrow or the next day and check it out.

Brad put the papers down. Maybe he could interest CJ in going. No, he reasoned, it was still too early to expect that. He would ask, but if she turned him down, it would still be all right.

Brad's concentration was completely broken. He tried three times to turn his attention back to the papers, but it was impossible. Getting up, he walked to the french doors that opened onto his balcony. The night air was cold and assaulted his skin through the silk pajamas he wore.

Staring out across the moonlit valley to the shadowed mountains in the distance, Brad prayed. "God," he began, "I love her. I think I've loved her from the first minute I saw her. I tried to do as Roger suggested, I really did. I think we have a good friendship, but Father, I want much more. I want to love CJ in the way that she needs to be loved, but the past

107

still stands between us. Help her, please, to deal with the pain and the things that haunt her mind. Heal her and make her whole, and God," Brad paused, concentrating hard on the words he would pray, "if it's Your will. . .let CJ be the one I'll marry. Amen."

The whispered prayer seemed to catch on the night winds, drifting out across the open land and ever upward to the starry heavens. Brad stood there for a long time, watching and wondering. How would he know? How would he know for sure if it was right to marry CJ?

❧

Mondays were devoted to cleaning house, at least for CJ. Monday was the day she put everything in order—her house and her emotions. It was also the day she saw Roger Prescott and walked back through time to the moments that had held her prisoner for so many years.

CJ smiled to herself as she opened the glass doors of the administrative building where Roger's office was. Today, she decided, would be her last visit. She'd come so far in the few months since she'd met Brad and Roger. It was hard to imagine the woman who'd existed back then, and CJ had no desire to dwell on her too much.

"You look as though you have the world by the tail," Roger said when CJ entered the room.

CJ's smile broadened. "I guess I feel that way, too."

"I take it the weekends are working out well and that flying hasn't caused you any problems," he said, casually opening their session.

CJ smoothed the skirt of her navy jumper and took a seat. "I feel wonderful, and I can't thank you and Brad enough. I guess I never realized what I was missing in life until Brad forced me to face it head on."

"And you feel now that you've put it all behind you?"

CJ toyed with the burgundy bow that trimmed her print blouse. "I know things aren't completely perfect, but I'm working on it."

"It's good that you still see room for improvement. God doesn't want us to stagnate." Roger paused, then changed the subject. "What about you and Brad? He tells me that he stepped outside the boundaries of friendship and lost his heart to you." Roger's face showed the delight he held for his friend. "How do you feel about that?"

"I'm not sure," CJ responded. "No, that's not true. It thrills me to pieces and scares me to death."

"Do you want to talk about it?"

"No," CJ said, shaking her head. "I don't think so. It's too new and I'm not sure what I feel or what to do with it."

"All right." Roger smiled and leaned back in his chair. "I know you've been coming regularly to the Bible study. Have you found it helpful?"

CJ nodded. "I know it's helped tremendously. I lost a good portion of guilt the day I realized I could never be good enough or do enough to earn my salvation."

"Guilt has played a heavy role in your life, hasn't it?"

Roger's words impacted CJ in a strange way. She really hadn't considered the guilt aspect for a very long time. "There was a time," she said in a faraway voice, "when I felt guilty for being alive. No matter what I did or how I looked at life, I was alive and they weren't, and for that I felt somehow to blame."

"Why?" Roger asked softly.

"You tell me." CJ laughed nervously. "You're the shrink."

Roger smiled. "You know it doesn't work that way."

"I guess I do." She paused and shifted in the seat to cross her legs. "Life is difficult to understand. I guess no one would dispute that." She didn't wait for Roger to comment, before moving on. "Still, it seems odd that a sixteen-year-old girl could take so much on her shoulders. I hated being left behind. I hated feeling the loss and knowing that everyone looked at me as the survivor of the crash that took Douglas O'Sullivan from the world. I wasn't a survivor." CJ slowly added, "In many ways, I was just as much a fatality of the crash as they were."

"And now?" Roger questioned.

"Now?" CJ shrugged. "Now, I'm not sure. I don't feel the same guilt, and the loss is easier to deal with. I'm more mature in my thinking and realize that of course the world would mourn my father while paying little attention to me."

"But?" Roger pressed.

"But?" CJ repeated the question.

"But there's something more. At least, that's how it sounded to me," Roger replied.

CJ swallowed hard. "I guess there is. I guess somewhere out there, there's a little girl still wandering around, trying to piece her life back together."

"Do you ever try to picture her?" Roger asked.

"What?" CJ asked, sounding surprised.

"Picture her. See yourself at sixteen again. What do you see?"

CJ closed her eyes. She focused on the girl she saw herself as before the crash. "I'm naive. I believe the world is a good place and that nothing can hurt me. I'm happy because I don't know that there is anything more than what I'm experiencing, and what I'm living is wonderful in my mind." CJ fell silent and felt tears come to her eyes.

"Go on, CJ. Tell me what else you see."

"I can't," she whispered.

"Is that where you want to leave her. . .naive, happy, living a wonderful life? Is she safe there?" Roger questioned.

"No," CJ answered and opened her eyes. "She's not safe. She's just waiting for the other shoe to drop."

"What do you mean?"

"She. . ." CJ shook her head, "I loved them so much. My folks were everything to me. My brother, too. Then one day, they just got into an airplane and flew out of my life. Even Curt flew away."

"And now you're afraid to give your heart to Brad because he just might do the same thing?"

CJ's eyes opened wide in surprise. "The other shoe," she whispered. "I never saw it that way before."

"Now that you do, what do you want to do about it?"

"I don't know," CJ said and shifted again in the seat. "I thought I was coming here today to tell you I was finished with these sessions. Now I don't think I will."

"It's up to you, CJ. You alone know when they stop being helpful. Some people rely on counseling for years and eventually it becomes as much a crutch as other things do. If you want to keep coming, I'm here. If you're ready to move on, that's fine, too."

CJ shook her head. "I thought the physical aspect of flying was my biggest problem to overcome. That and my anger at God. Now I see a whole new slate of problems, and I guess I'm confused. I can't stop now and leave in the middle." With a weak smile, she looked up at Roger. "It'd be too much like putting down a good book before reading the last chapter."

Roger laughed. "You're just beginning to write that book, CJ. You won't reach the last earthly chapter until God calls you home."

When the session ended, Roger walked with CJ out to her car. The air was colder than it had been the day before and CJ wished she'd thought to bring her jacket.

"CJ," Roger said as she unlocked her door. "I'd like to say something, but not as a counselor. . .just as a friend."

"Go ahead," CJ replied, a look of curiosity punctuating her words.

Roger shoved his hands into his pants pockets and smiled in a sheepish way. "I've known Brad a while now, and I don't mind saying he's a good guy. He's participated in the church with more enthusiasm than most, and any time there's a special project, he's more than willing to do his part. And," Roger added with a wink, "the single gals have been mighty disappointed to see him devote so much time to you."

CJ laughed but wondered what Roger was getting at. Roger grew quiet for a moment, then looked past CJ to the mountains. "I guess what I want to tell you is that he's worthy of your trust. I know I warned him not to fall in love with you, but you have to understand, that was purely on a professional level. Frankly, I knew he was already headed there when we talked, but I didn't want him to concentrate on the love interest so much that he protected you from dealing with the real issue of your fear. If I wronged you in that, I hope you'll forgive me."

CJ reached out and put her hand on Roger's arm. "I don't believe you wronged me at all. I wasn't ready to fall in love, then. I'm not even sure about now, but I do know that I cherish the friendship I have with Brad and I think it makes a good foundation for whatever else might come."

Roger nodded. "You're pretty smart, CJ O'Sullivan."

❧

The phone was ringing as CJ opened the door to her apartment. Juggling groceries, she answered breathlessly.

"Hi, thought I'd check in with you."

"Brad! Where are you? Did you have to fly back from Jackson Hole in the storm?" CJ sounded panicked.

"What storm?" Brad asked. Thunder crashed loudly, and before CJ could reply, Brad's voice answered nonchalantly, "Oh, that storm."

"Where are you?" CJ asked again.

"Wyoming. By the time my meeting ended, it was too late to fly back, so I decided to give my own hotel a try."

CJ sighed and sounded much relieved when she spoke. "I was worried. I kept watching that storm move in from the north and I just knew you'd be foolish enough to try and beat it in."

"Never worry about things like that CJ," Brad assured. "I take my flight safety very seriously. I've seen too many things go wrong to chance it. In fact, I'm probably over cautious."

"Good. Keep it that way."

"You growing fond of me or something?

CJ laughed. "Or something," she replied. Another loud crash of thunder rocked the panes in her windows. "It sure is a nasty storm for this time of year. I was totally surprised. One minute the weather was perfect; the next thing I knew I was nearly drenched. I was outside, bringing in groceries, when you called."

"Where's Cheryl?"

"She was supposed to meet Stratton. I hope he kept the date. He's sure treated her strangely here lately. I think Cheryl's honestly questioning whether she'll marry him at all."

"Marriage is an important commitment," Brad remarked.

CJ found the opportunity to discuss the subject too tempting to ignore. "That's what I told Cheryl," she began, using Cheryl to distance herself from harm. "I told her she needed to be able to trust Stratton with her life, as well as her emotions. If he doesn't look out for her overall well-being, then he just doesn't care the way he should."

"I think that's a very important point. You should probably tell Cheryl, as well, that most men find women somewhat of a mystery. She should be straightforward with him and let him know exactly what she expects out of marriage."

"True," CJ said, knowing that Brad realized her game. "A man should be no different. Say for instance, he expects a wife to give up all her other interests in life for his, he should tell her before they walk down the aisle together."

"Or if he'd just like to see her get some interests in life," Brad retorted.

"Well, maybe if she had problems that kept her from seeking outside influences, then she'd be justified in having very few interests. But I think she's working that all out." CJ realized how stupid she sounded and laughed. "After all, Cheryl went to the art gallery with me just yesterday, and she told me that she thought my art history degree would be best put to use in owning my own gallery."

"An art gallery, huh?" Brad questioned. "I didn't know you even had an interest in such a thing."

"There's a lot about me you don't know," CJ quipped. A quick glance out the kitchen window showed that the storm was abating.

"Guess I'd better be straightforward then."

"I guess you'd better." CJ liked their coded banter. "Now tell me, how did your meeting go?"

"Pretty well," Brad admitted. They talked on for several minutes about his plans, when suddenly CJ realized he'd not had supper.

"You'd better go get something to eat," she stated firmly.

"Yes, dear," he replied in a teasing voice.

"And if you're flying back at the crack of dawn, you'll want to get to bed early."

"Yes, dear."

"Just being straightforward," CJ replied with a laugh.

"Yes, dear." Brad's voice betrayed his amusement. "Good night, dear."

"Good night," CJ said, then quickly added, "Brad?"

"Yeah?"

"Thanks for letting me know you were all right. Be careful tomorrow." There was no teasing in her voice.

"I will be. Don't worry, just pray."

With a smile, Brad hung up the phone. "She loves me," he whispered to the room. "She doesn't realize it yet, but she loves me." He patted his chest in a self-satisfied way and whistled while he browsed through the room service menu. Things were definitely looking up.

fourteen

Brad's trip home was delayed when a heavy rain and overcast skies developed in the night and continued through the next day. Clear skies finally came late the next morning, and Brad flew out for Denver shortly before noon. He questioned the sensibility of leaving that late. Turbulence over the mountains would be greater as the day wore on and the temperatures warmed the air. But he wanted to be home more than anything else in the world.

Hours later he dialed the now familiar number. "Honey, I'm home," he said in a teasing, singsong voice.

"Brad?" CJ said in a questioning tone.

"Who else would call you honey?" Brad asked earnestly. "There isn't anyone else, is there?"

CJ smiled. "Now why would I tell you, if there were?"

Brad sobered a bit, realizing that it was suddenly very important to him that he be the only man in CJ's life. "What happened to being straightforward? There isn't anyone else, is there?" His voice took on a pleading note.

A strange sensation overcame CJ. "No, you know there isn't." Her voice was completely serious.

Brad exhaled in relief. "Good. Now, let's keep it that way."

"Sounds kind of possessive," CJ replied.

"I feel very possessive when it comes to you. I think I'm only coming to realize how important you are to me. I kept thinking about you all the time I was in Jackson, and I couldn't keep my mind on what I was doing."

"Now that sounds dangerous. I hope you were concentrating on the plane when you were flying back home."

Brad laughed. "Well, most of the time. Say, can you come over?"

CJ glanced at the clock. "Right now?"

"Sure. Come on out and I'll fix my famous Chicken à la Brad and we can have a nice cozy fire. Maybe we could watch some mushy, romantic movie and I could tell you how wonderful you are and you could tell me—"

"How wonderful you are," CJ filled in. "All right. You talked me into it. Can I bring anything?"

"Just yourself. That's really all I want." Brad's words sent out a clear message.

❧

CJ rang the bell and waited for Brad to open the door. She was grateful for the wool coat she'd thought to wear and hugged it close against the unseasonably cold breezes. Was it more than the wind that made her tremble? Seeing Brad again was more than a little exciting. She wondered nervously if she'd be able to act reasonably.

It's been only two days, she chided herself. But, for some reason, it had been two very important days. Deep down, CJ had come to realize she cared quite deeply for Brad.

Brad opened the door, wearing a broad smile. "How good of you to come, Miss O'Sullivan." He bowed low and stepped back.

"Good of you to have me, Mr. Aldersson."

Brad took her coat and hung it up. When he turned back around, he pulled CJ into his arms. With a sigh, she melted against him. She lifted her face to his and let her arms travel up his, until her hands met behind his neck. For the first time, CJ initiated their kiss, pulling his face down to meet hers. Brad didn't hesitate for a moment.

"I love you so very much, CJ O'Sullivan," Brad whispered

against her ear.

CJ smiled and put her head against his sweatered chest. She wanted to return his words, but the image Roger had concocted of Brad, flying away, came back to haunt her. She was suddenly afraid and pulled back rather quickly.

"What's wrong?" Brad asked, fearing that he'd done something to offend her.

"Nothing. Honestly, nothing at all," CJ protested, knowing she sounded startled. Before Brad could press her further, CJ threw up her hands. "It's just my insecurities. Please, bear with me."

Brad reached out and pulled her back to him. "Come on, I have a nice fire crackling away on the grate and no one to enjoy it with."

They sat and talked for hours and at one point Brad served them dinner on a checkered tablecloth on the floor in front of the fireplace.

CJ kicked off her boots and relaxed against the coffee table, while Brad cleared away the dishes. It was nice to be cared for in such a completely giving way. In the back of her mind, however, a thought struck CJ. Brad was doing all the giving, and she, in her needy way, was taking all that he offered.

Feeling guilty, CJ patted the space beside her when Brad returned with coffee. "I'm afraid I should apologize," she began. "You've done so much for me this evening, and I've done very little for you."

Brad smiled provocatively and put the coffee on the table behind CJ. "I can think of many ways you could repay me," he whispered, kneeling beside her.

CJ smiled. "So can I, but most of them are totally inappropriate, and I think maybe I should go home."

Brad laughed. "Relax, you're safe with me. I honor the same values and principles you do, remember?"

"Yes," CJ mused, "but it's difficult at times like this to remember just what all those principles are."

"Good point," Brad said solemnly. "I think our relationship is coming to the place where we need to make some important decisions."

CJ lowered her head. "I don't know if I can."

Brad reached out and ran a finger along CJ's jaw. It came to rest under her chin, lifting her face to meet his. "I'm not asking you to marry me, at least not just yet. But I would like a commitment between us. Something I can count on as solid and trustworthy."

"I thought we already had that," CJ whispered.

"In a sense, but I just want to know that you belong to me. Does that sound terribly chauvinistic?"

"Terribly," CJ said with a slow, sweet smile. "But I like it, and you can count on it, as far as I'm concerned. There's no one else I'm interested in, nor do I desire to be this close to anyone but you."

☙

Friday night, Brad called to tell CJ to bring an overnight bag for their flight the following morning.

"What do you have planned?" CJ questioned. "We've never gone flying anywhere that would require we stay over. I'm not sure I'm up to the distance and—"

"Nonsense," Brad interrupted. "I have to go up to Jackson, and I want you to come with me. It will be the perfect time for you to put your fears to rest, once and for all. We'll have fun, CJ, and we can stay at the resort and go swimming or sightseeing. . .whatever you want to do."

"I don't know," CJ said apprehensively.

"Well, I do and, if I have to, I'll come pack you, myself. Now, take warm clothes and meet me at the hangar at six."

"Okay," she said, getting her courage up. "I'll go."

"You promise?"

"Promise."

CJ faced her decision with a great deal of turmoil. It shouldn't bother so much, but it did. When morning came, she got up before the sun, wrote out a note for Cheryl who hadn't returned the night before, and took off for the airport.

"Please, Father," she prayed as she drove up to park beside Brad's Jeep. "Please give me the strength and courage I need for this day. Amen."

When she looked up, Brad stood in the doorway of the hangar. For a moment, all CJ could do was stare. He was gorgeous. *He is everything a man should be,* she thought. Tall and tanned. Brown hair glinting gold from the sun, blowing in the light breeze. Passionate, intense eyes that seemed to stare through to her soul. He wore insulated flight coveralls, and a ball cap with "O&F Aviation" written across it was in his hands. It was the company CJ's father had co-owned with Cheryl's.

Shyly she stepped out of the car, thinking the scene looked like something out of the movies. As if sensing his effect on her, a lopsided grin broke the serious expression on his face.

"Welcome to Aldersson Airlines. I have insulated coveralls for you inside. I'm going to finish the preflight check," he said, taking her bag. "I'm on the backside of the hangar. Just come on around when you're dressed."

CJ nodded and did as she was told, grateful for the extra warmth of the one-piece suit. Brad had just completed his inspection when she came around the corner and spotted the plane. CJ froze. It was a replica of her parents' plane—the same one that had taken them from her.

She felt the color drain from her face. The blue and white

Cessna greeted her like an apparition from the past.

"I thought if you were going to put this behind you once and for all, we might as well put you in the same kind of plane. I know I should have told you, but honestly, CJ, it's no different than the Travel Air. It's just an airplane," Brad said firmly.

CJ stared at the Cessna as though she expected her parents to wave back from the cockpit. "I can't do this," she said and turned to leave.

"Yes, you can," Brad insisted, and his arm shot out to stop her flight. "It's just a bad memory. That's all it is. Your parents are in heaven, safe and happy. You have to put this to rest. You have to let go of that accident."

CJ leaned her back against Brad's chest and took a deep breath. Dread overwhelmed her in a tidal wave of emotion. Trembling and weak-kneed, she nodded. "I know you're right. I want to let go. I truly do."

"Then fly with me today and give it over to God. It's only two hours and forty minutes to Jackson. You can do it, CJ. I know you can, and you know God can help you do it. Remember Philippians 4:13."

"I can do everything through him who gives me strength," CJ whispered in reply.

"That's right. Everything. . .through Christ." Brad's words neutralized her fears. "You'll work in Christ's strength, CJ. Not your own."

Pushing Brad's arms aside, CJ squared her shoulders and turned to face both Brad and the plane. "Everything through Christ," she repeated. "Everything."

fifteen

Even climbing into the plane caused a rush of memories to fill CJ's mind. She eyed the cockpit knowingly. She'd flown in her father's Cessna 182 many times. Now, here she was, in the one place she'd vowed never to be again.

CJ could very nearly see her father in the pilot's seat beside her. She could almost hear her mother's laughter as they prepared to go on one of their many adventures.

"Are you okay?" Brad's voice broke through the madness.

"Uh-huh," she murmured with a slight nod of her head.

Brad checked over a self-made list and radioed out on common frequency to begin their journey. CJ was lost again in thought. Voices from the past filled her head. It was her father making the radio announcement of takeoff, not Brad. It was his smiling face that looked over at her.

"CJ, you look as white as a ghost. Are you going to be sick? CJ?" Brad reached over and touched her hand.

She looked up. "I'm fine. Really. Just a lot of memories to work through."

Brad nodded and moved the aircraft down the runway. In a matter of seconds, they were airborne, and only then did CJ realize she'd been holding her breath the entire time. Exhaling loudly, she tried to ignore Brad's grin.

"You're still alive and well," he said, trying to lighten her spirits. "You may as well relax and enjoy the view."

CJ tried. The day was perfect, and the air was clear and cold. She could see for miles around her in the cloudless sky. The mountains glimmered from their new toppings of snow, and CJ reminded herself how comforting these majestic markers had always been in her life.

"Life is like climbing those peaks," her father had told her. "You see only your side of the mountain, and while you climb and trudge through, there is no other side. But once you get to the top, you can look down around you and see where you came from and where you're going to. When we're in the valleys, just climbing out and up, we can't believe there will ever be that viewpoint. Just remember it, though, and don't get discouraged when things get hard. Climb to the top, CJ. The view from there is fantastic!"

She nodded to herself as though the voice had reached across the years. Her father and mother had taught her so much about living. They'd truly hate knowing that she'd spent so much of her young life focused on death. Especially their deaths.

CJ glanced over at Brad. He was perfectly at ease doing his favorite job. He loved to fly and had told her so on many occasions. Once or twice when they'd talked about flying, CJ had allowed herself to remember the way it felt.

Her eyes moved from Brad to the dual control in front of her. It moved with unison rhythm as Brad maneuvered them through the air. She reached out a finger and let it ride on the control, just feeling the pulsating moves.

Brad looked over and smiled. "You want to give it a try?"

CJ pulled her hand back as though she'd touched a flame. "No!" she exclaimed more quickly than she'd intended. Calming her nerves, she smiled. "I was just remembering."

"You really ought to get your pilot's license. You could become involved with your father's enterprise again, instead of letting Curt run things by proxy."

"Even Curt doesn't spend that much time with it. Cheryl's father has everything under control. The air show business isn't what it used to be. It's much more complicated, and that, coupled with the way the aviation company has grown, makes me pretty useless. It's probably best that I stay out of it. Maybe I'll open that art gallery like Cheryl suggested."

"Think you could be happy, grounded?" Brad questioned. "You are Doug O'Sullivan's daughter, after all. Five years without the things you cut your teeth on are bound to have taken their toll in more than the obvious ways. I think you love all of this as much as he did."

CJ recoiled a bit into the seat. Love the thing that killed her parents? "That was before," she murmured.

"Before the crash, you mean?"

"Yes," CJ answered. "I doubt my father would think too highly of this profession now."

"You mean if he'd lived through the crash, as you did?"

"Exactly."

Brad laughed and surprised CJ even more. "You don't remember your father very well then. CJ, he went through a dozen near misses and minor crashes. He even experienced a pretty bad one during the war. You should know. He teetered between life and death for weeks."

"I don't know what you're talking about," CJ replied in complete shock. "Sure, Daddy had some risky moments, but I don't know anything about an accident like what you're telling me about."

Brad shook his head. "I'm sorry. I didn't know. They must have kept it from you. It happened before you were born. My point, however, is that Doug knew the risks related to flying, and after each disaster, he got back into the cockpit and did it all over again. The last accident wouldn't have kept Doug O'Sullivan grounded, even if it had taken the lives of those he loved. Flying was his life, and you, your mother, and brother were all a part of it."

CJ looked at Brad as though she couldn't believe the words he spoke. "I know he loved flying, but I can't imagine wanting to be a part of something that took away those you cared for so deeply."

Brad's expression softened. "Ignoring the pleasures of something you love to do wouldn't bring them back. It's no different for you, now. Just because you won't pilot a plane, doesn't balance out the fact that they can't be here with you. Let them go, CJ. They aren't far away, and you'll see them again. Just let it all go."

CJ grew quiet and turned to stare out the window as if by doing so, she could block out Brad's words. She hated the logic of it all. Why was it so hard to admit that she'd buffered herself for years behind the false assumption that her parents would have reacted the same way?

❧

The trip to Jackson was perfect. The winds were cooperative and turbulence was low. Even when they had to fly close to dangerous ridges and downdrafts, Brad was able to position the plane in such a way that they sailed through, high above, without difficulties.

CJ had never been to Jackson Hole before, and she enjoyed the time they shared there. The scenery was spectacular with the rugged Teton peaks rising heavenward. Already dressed in heavy snowcaps, they looked much more rustic than CJ's beloved mountains in Colorado.

The view from her hotel room was impressive, and CJ enjoyed relaxing there when Brad left for his meeting with the real estate agent. He was quite optimistic about his purchase, and CJ was happy that his plans were coming together. As she stretched out on the queen-sized bed, she daydreamed about what it would be like if Brad's plans and aspirations were her own.

The thought was a pleasant one, and CJ giggled to herself in little-girl fashion, all the while contemplating what it might be like to be Mrs. Brad Aldersson. Then a cloud of frustration shadowed the fantasy. Brad would no doubt continue to fly all over the country, especially if his resorts expanded in the manner he hoped. She'd have to fly with him or be left home a great deal of the time. Maybe he'd even expect her to get her pilot's license and help with the flying.

Her mind raced with images of treacherous mountain blizzards and freak thunderstorms. She could imagine the tiny Cessna or twin-engine Beech being tossed mercilessly through the air. Shaking her head, CJ forced the picture from her mind.

"Oh, Brad," she sighed. "If I love you, will I always have to confront this thing?"

If I love you? CJ laughed aloud. She knew full well that it was too late. She already did love Brad Aldersson, she just couldn't find the words to tell him. Then, too, maybe she was afraid of what would happen once she made that declaration. Would he push her to marry immediately? Did she want that?

That evening, she enjoyed his company, with guarded emotions. Brad was the exuberant new owner of prime acreage in Jackson Hole. They celebrated in grand style at the finest restaurant in town, then slowly made their way back to the hotel.

"Weather still looks good for tomorrow's flight," Brad stated, walking CJ to her door. "There's a cold front moving in, but it's dragging a bit, so we've got plenty of time. I've got someone watching the weather, and they'll give me a call if the conditions deteriorate."

CJ tried to approach the subject enthusiastically. "I hope

the return trip is as wonderful as the one coming up. Everything was so pretty and—"

Brad put a finger to her lips. "Don't. You don't have to pretend with me. I know you're afraid, but I'll take every precaution to ensure that we stay safe."

"Daddy did that, too," CJ argued softly.

Brad smiled and pulled her into his arms. "Yes, he did. But God called him home, and when He calls us, it will be no different. We'll be ready to go and walk jubilantly into the arms of our Savior. Is there any fear in that?"

CJ trembled in his arms, and a single tear slid down her cheek. "But what if it only takes one of us? What then?"

Brad kissed the wet spot on her face. "Either God is God, or He isn't. We trust, and we go on. We live life and expect the best in His Will for us. There are no guarantees, CJ, except that through Christ, we defeat death."

CJ felt a bit of peace in his words. She knew Brad was right. She had to let God be in control. She had to let go of the past, her fears, and her worries. But how very hard it was to trust!

❧

That night CJ dreamed she was falling. The ground raced up to meet her, but she never came to a stop. She just kept falling and falling. Pain in her left leg woke her up once. She shifted positions and fell back asleep, thinking of how the old dream never seemed to fade from her mind.

Around five-thirty in the morning, her phone rang. "Sorry to wake you, CJ, but the front's picked up speed and there's another behind it. I'd suggest we wait it out, but from the looks of it, we could be here a while."

"So what other choice do we have?" CJ asked in a sleepy voice.

"We leave right now," Brad replied. "The weather's good

and by the time we get up and running, it'll be light. Can you be ready to go in five minutes?"

CJ came awake instantly. "Sure. I'll meet you downstairs."

"No, I'll come get you. I don't want you wandering around the hotel by yourself at this hour." Brad's protectiveness made CJ feel good. "Just stay put. I'll be over shortly."

CJ scurried around the room, grateful that she'd thought to pack everything the night before. She pulled on her blue jeans and tucked in a dark green tee shirt before pulling a heavy wool sweater over her head. Grimacing, she didn't even take time to put on makeup and was just doing up the laces on her hiking boots when Brad knocked on the doorway.

"I'm ready," she said, thrusting her bag through the door into Brad's waiting arms.

"What? No good morning kiss?" Brad teased.

CJ leaned across the bag and placed a light kiss on Brad's lips. "Good morning," she said. She pushed her hair back only to realize that she'd forgotten to brush it. "Oh, no!" she exclaimed. "My hair must look frightful. Well, this is the best you get with a five-minute warning. No makeup and no combed out hair." She shrugged good-naturedly and stared up into Brad's twinkling eyes.

"You look fine," Brad said with a wink. "I kind of like it all tossed around like that."

CJ rolled her eyes. "Just let me borrow your cap, okay?"

Brad laughed out loud, forgetting the hour. He quieted down when CJ put a finger to her lips. Shifting the bag, he pulled the baseball cap from his jacket pocket and handed it to her.

"Are you ready now, or is there something else you want before we go?" he asked with a sardonic grin.

"Breakfast would have been nice," she countered.

"I've already arranged for the kitchen to have something

waiting for us to take along. We can pick it up on our way out."

CJ shook her head and reached out to open the unzipped front of Brad's coat.

"What are you doing?" His confusion was apparent.

"Just looking."

"For what?" Brad questioned in earnest.

"Your cape," CJ replied.

"My cape?"

"Your hero cape. You know. . .Superhero Brad! Defender of the weak! Nourisher of the hungry! Pilot for the cowardly!"

It was Brad's turn to roll his eyes, and with a low chuckle he asked, "Are you finished?

CJ adjusted the cap, pushing her long red hair inside. "Yes, Super Brad," she replied. "Lead on."

❧

Brad made an engine run-up and double checked to make certain the radio was on the 123.0 frequency for Jackson Hole.

"Jackson Hole traffic," he announced on the common frequency, "this is Cessna Four-Kilo-Mike departing runway One-niner."

CJ tensed in the seat as Brad moved the craft down the runway. They lifted gracefully into the air, and once again CJ felt relieved to see they were up and on their way. It was more the anticipation of the thing that bothered her.

Brad turned the plane to the right and radioed once again. "Jackson Hole traffic, Cessna Four-Kilo-Mike departing to the east." He replaced the mike and turned to CJ. "Look, we're greeting the morning." He pointed to the rush of color that lit up the eastern horizon.

CJ watched as he maneuvered the plane and climbed to 9,500 feet. Leveling off, Brad seemed relaxed and content, almost like an extension of the Cessna. *He loves it,* CJ thought. He was just like her father. Sitting back, CJ finally gave into her fatigue and dozed.

The first turbulence hit them about the same time Brad was contemplating the breakfast they'd brought along. He contacted the nearest flight service station and updated the altimeter setting before making a climb to calmer air space. CJ instantly awoke at the disturbance, but Brad assured her all was well.

"We just passed the cabins at Fremont Lake," he announced. We're up to 13,500 and things seem a little calmer here. Hungry?"

She shook her head. The nerves in her stomach were suddenly tight. "No, I think I'll wait."

"There's a thermos of coffee back there. Maybe that would help settle your stomach."

She looked at him wonderingly and again shook her head. "I'm fine. You want me to get you something?"

"Yeah, I think they packed some donuts and I don't know what else," he replied. He started humming while CJ frowned ever so slightly.

"What's that song?" she asked, unbuckling herself.

" 'Have a Little Talk With Jesus,' " Brad sang out just as the plane lurched.

"Looks like you'd better have more than a little talk," CJ suggested.

Brad laughed while CJ reached around behind his seat to where the small box of food had been placed. The plane bumped up and down, causing CJ to lose her grip on the plastic thermos. It rolled back behind her and wedged out of reach. She watched the skies, with a sense of dread. To the east was the Wind River Mountain Range, with it's twelve- and thirteen-thousand-foot peaks. It seemed most intimidating to CJ. Even worse was the fading visibility to the south.

"On second thought," Brad said, trying not to appear overly concerned, "I think I'll wait on that donut."

CJ nodded, buckled herself back in, and resumed her vigil of the skies. Things weren't good, and there was no way Brad could keep it from her. She was, after all, Douglas O'Sullivan's daughter. She'd grown up in planes and probably had logged more air miles than most pilots.

They covered another one hundred miles or so before Brad radioed for another updated setting. It was critical for a pilot to keep track of the local pressure in order to reset the altimeter. Otherwise, he might actually believe he was at one altitude when, in fact, he could be much lower. Flying over mountain terrain made this little inconvenience even more important.

CJ sat in silence while Brad and flight service discussed the changing weather. It seemed the easterly front, which had been expected to move through by this time, had stalled out over Denver and built back.

Brad weighed his options. Very few existed. Visual Flight Rules, or VFR, required a three-mile visibility, and Jackson Hole was now socked in with the low pressure system pushing forward and picking up speed. Turning back was out of the question.

Finally, a course was plotted that would take them over some rough mountain terrain, but even then Brad wasn't worried. He'd flown the area many times before and anticipated the dangers in advance—at least as much in advance as mountain flying allowed for. They'd simply fly high and take no chances.

Things seemed to settle down for a time, and although problems existed, CJ tried to remind herself that Brad was a capable and experienced flyer. With a wing and a prayer, they'd surely get through, wasn't that what her father had always said?

They passed the miles in silence, but eventually Brad seemed to sensed her tension worsening and he reached across with a quick pat on her arm.

"A walk in the park," he teased, knowing that CJ knew full well how bad things could get.

"Right," she replied and sarcastically added, "you could probably do it with your eyes closed."

"Not and fly VFR," Brad laughed. The plane jumped a bit and settled back down. CJ's knuckles were white from gripping the edge of the seat.

"Relax," Brad tried to encourage. "Remember what the Luke 4:10 says, 'He will command his angels concerning you, to guard you carefully.' Maybe He could stake one or two under the wings."

"I wonder if angels have to worry about turbulence and downdrafts," CJ quipped.

Brad laughed. "Just keep your sense of humor, honey. We'll be fine."

The word "fine" was barely out his mouth when the plane ran into another bouncing bout with the elements. It reminded CJ of a roller coaster ride, and she worried for a brief moment that she'd get sick.

Brad had worries of his own when Mt. Zirkel came into view after they crossed into Colorado airspace. He checked the altimeter. At 13,500 feet, he should be well above the landmark, but for some reason the mountain looked much higher than usual. Maybe CJ's paranoia was getting to him. He glanced over and gave her a smile.

Heading toward the Bow Mountain Range, Brad tried to make radio contact, but received only static. He was quickly reaching the point where he'd have to make serious decisions on his own.

"We're going to go higher," he told CJ. She only nodded and cowered into her corner. Brad felt badly that he couldn't cajole or comfort her in the midst of the frightening situation, but he had his hands full and his mind was more than a little bit preoccupied.

The plane fought to pick up altitude, while the wind campaigned in equal earnest to push it back down. To CJ, the plane seemed too frail to endure much more. She alternated between pleading with God and raging against Him at the injustice of it all.

All of a sudden, a tremendous blow came against them, and CJ knew they were falling from the sky. The plane kept plummeting with Brad working at the controls to somehow achieve the lift they needed. Nothing worked.

"You'd better get down," Brad said with an authoritative sternness that left CJ no hope that he'd recover the descent.

CJ shook her head. This just couldn't be happening. How could God be so cruel as to make her go through it again?

"I love you, Brad!" she exclaimed, knowing that if she didn't say it now, she might never get a chance.

Brad laughed. "Now you tell me."

The mountain peaks rushed up to meet them, then something miraculous happened and Brad managed to pull them up just a bit. It was too late to keep them from crashing, but they had more control, and he banked them ever so diligently toward an open valley.

"Get down!" Brad ordered, and CJ quickly complied.

"Dear God," she whispered, "forgive me my sins and deliver us from death." Her mind drifted into the memory of another crash. "He's done us in, Jan," she suddenly remembered her father saying, just before the noise of the crash tore through the plane. *Oh God,* she thought, *I don't want to die.* It was her last conscious thought.

sixteen

The landing gear broke up and scattered across the mountain. Brad fought for some kind of control and quickly realized there was little to be had. When they finally skidded to a stop, the plane had flipped several times and finally landed upside down.

Brad, though dazed, never lost consciousness. He was aware of a burning pain in his side and the fact that he was half lying, half hanging against the cockpit door. The haze gradually lifted from his mind, and the cold of the snow-spotted valley brought him fully awake.

"CJ!" he cried her name and fought the harness that bound him to the cockpit seat.

The wreckage left Brad frustrated as he struggled to free himself. CJ was unconscious. A trickle of blood marred her otherwise peaceful looking face. Sometime during the crash, she'd lost his baseball cap, and now copper hair spilled out everywhere in tangled disarray.

"CJ!" Brad said her name over and over, trying to evoke some response as he managed to free himself.

He knew without checking that she was alive. CJ's rhythmic breathing confirmed his assumptions. Remembering the bit of control he had over the plane right before the crash, Brad felt certain that God had brought them both through for a purpose. But what could it possibly be?

Working CJ's jammed seat belt, Brad freed her and pulled her from the wreckage. Tenderly, he put her on the ground several feet from the fuselage and looked around to survey the damage.

The plane looked like a turtle, stranded on its back. The landing gear had been ripped away and the wing on one side was lying at an angle. It was a miracle that they were alive.

Still a bit stunned, Brad managed to locate one of the blankets he'd kept in the plane. He spread it out on the ground next to CJ, and then gently rolled her onto it. He gave her a cursory going-over to see if she was injured. There were no stains of crimson to give him reason for concern, and Brad sat down hard, sighing with relief. The bump on her head had already begun to turn purple, but the bleeding was barely noticeable.

Twisting around to get his bearings, Brad cried out in pain. His hand went to his side, where something had punctured him during the crash. He unzipped his coveralls and reached in his hand, bringing it out bloody. Struggling to his feet, he went to search the fuselage for their bags and the first-aid kit.

The winds picked up, and heavy clouds began to lower over the valley while Brad worked to find their things in the jumbled mess. He tried the radio to no avail and glanced again to the sky. Hopefully the ELT, Emergency Locator Transmitter, would already be sending out signals that someone flying overhead could pick up. Brad silently thanked God he'd taken the time to file a flight plan and that the flight service knew their whereabouts after their last altimeter update. It would greatly reduce the time in locating them.

Pulling together what he could, Brad managed to dress his wound and stop the bleeding. His next concern was CJ. When he knelt beside her, she was already coming to.

In her mind, CJ was sixteen again. She felt the pain and the fear. The smell of fuel assailed her nose and, for the first time since the accident, she could see the twisted, bleeding bodies of her parents.

"No!" she screamed. "Daddy, no!" She struggled to fight the wreckage and flailed her arms against its hold.

"CJ, calm down. It's okay. We're okay!" Brad said, holding her down.

CJ was unable to shake the image. "They're dead! They're dead! Somebody help me!"

"Shhh," Brad soothed and pulled her close. "It's all over, CJ. Wake up, honey."

CJ opened her eyes. The wreckage of her parents' plane was gone. Brad's concerned face replaced the horrors of contorted death. "What's happened?" she questioned in a whisper. Her mind refused to accept the accident they'd just endured.

"Rough landing," Brad quipped. CJ struggled to sit up, but Brad held her fast. "How's your head?"

"My head?" CJ questioned. "My head is fine. Why is it so cold?"

"Perhaps because we're on top of a mountain with a storm about to hit," Brad replied sarcastically, letting her sit up.

CJ stared around in disbelief. Then it all started to come back. The downdrafts. . .the plane going down. It was suddenly very clear.

"Oh, Brad!" she exclaimed and clung to him as though she were about to drown. She moaned his name over and over, while he held her tightly and stroked her hair.

"It's okay," he whispered. "We made it. God protected us through the crash. Are you hurt anywhere?"

CJ refused to answer his questions. She refused to let go. It was too much. How could God do this to her twice in one lifetime? *I trusted You, Lord,* she thought. *I trusted You.*

The wind picked up, a sure sign that the storm was nearly upon them. Brad knew if the weather continued to build, search and rescue would be unable to locate them, much less pick them up. He needed to make a shelter of some kind. Prying himself away from CJ's grip, he glanced around.

"CJ, we have to get to work. I have a feeling we're about to be pelted with rain or snow, and we've got to get out of the elements. I want you to try to stand and see if you're hurt."

"No, don't leave me. I can't bear it!" She reached out and grabbed him again.

"Honey, I'm not going anywhere. I just want to see if you're hurt, and if not, you can help me fix up a shelter." CJ was still unconvinced. She refused to loosen her hold on Brad.

He wanted to go on holding her—anything to take the fear from her eyes. Brad remembered Roger's words about love marring objectivity. Feeling cruel, he forced CJ away from him.

"We have to get to work. I'm serious, now." He hated himself for the words. "Stand up," he ordered, getting to his own feet. He refused to wince even though the pain in his side was more than he wanted to admit.

CJ stared up at him, from the ground. "No," she said, refusing to budge. "I won't. I can't."

"Yes, you can," Brad insisted and pulled her to her feet. "Now, walk around and see if anything hurts."

CJ glared at him for a moment, tossed her hair over her shoulder, and walked. Brad saw the rage in her face and felt the anger that was barely contained.

"Move your arms around," Brad said, watching her carefully.

CJ flapped them like a bird, with a scowl on her face. "If I were dying I wouldn't tell you. You're acting like a real . . ." She paused as if trying to think of something bad enough to call him. When nothing came, she simply retorted, "I'm fine!"

"Then why are you so mad?" he questioned with a grin.

"I'm not mad!" CJ yelled at him.

"Then why are you shouting?" The grin broadened into a smile.

His calm irritated her. "I just want to make sure you can hear me!" she yelled.

"I don't think it's that at all. You're mad. I think it's that Irish temper getting the better of you."

"I think you stubborn Swedes have the compassion and manners of goats! You're supposed to help me feel better. You know. . .comfort and kindness. I've just been through—"

"We've just been through," Brad interjected. "Stop feeling sorry for yourself. We're in this together."

CJ suddenly stopped her ranting. She was rather embarrassed to realize she was taking out her emotions on Brad. She looked him square in the face and felt her indignation fade away. "Oh, Brad," she breathed and came to him. Wrapping her arms around him, CJ heard him grunt when she tightened her hold. "You're hurt, aren't you?"

"It's nothing much. I've already taken care of it," Brad replied.

CJ stepped back in disbelief. She surveyed the blood-stained rips in the side of his coveralls. "Nothing much? Sure. People lose blood like that all the time."

Brad laughed. "Stop fretting. I promise to let you tend to it later. You can fuss all over me and tell me how brave I was and what a good pilot I am." His eyes were twinkling. "Right now, though," he said and turned her to face the craggy peaks behind them, "we've got to make a shelter."

CJ took a deep breath, nodding at the heavy, gray sky. "Daddy always said, stay with the plane. People die because they wander away from the wreckage and get disoriented. Stay with the plane."

"What's left of it will hardly offer much comfort," Brad replied. "We won't venture far, though. Why don't you look around in the plane and find our things. Just make a pile so we can utilize what we have. I'll go scout out that rock face. Maybe we can hole up there."

CJ nodded and watched Brad cross over to the rocks. She looked at the angry, snow-heavy sky and then across to the man who'd managed to save her life. "Why, God?" she whispered. "Why this? Why now?" The wind whipped across her face with an icy chill, and CJ shivered. Suddenly she questioned everything. Her faith. Her life. Her death. How did it all figure together?

Rubbing her hands over her arms, CJ turned her attention to the plane and grimaced. She wondered how Brad had managed to keep it relatively in one piece. *He must be some kind of pilot*, she thought, then laughed nervously. Maybe angels had helped out.

CJ silently searched the plane, located their bags, and pulled them from the wreckage. After a little more investigation, she managed to turn up another blanket. Glancing around her, she suddenly realized that she couldn't see Brad anywhere. Apprehension gnawed at her shattered nerves. Where had he gone?

Standing alone on the mountain top, CJ was reminded of her father's analogy about mountain peaks. "You never told me, Daddy, what to do when the peaks were covered with clouds and you can't see behind you and you can't see ahead," CJ whispered to the wind.

The cold numbed her fingers, and CJ began to shake. Pacing in a circle to keep her blood circulating, the truth of what had happened began to sink in. They were stranded! Trapped on top of a rocky fortress. A most unforgiving one, at that.

CJ started to cry but pushed the tears back. Her throat ached from the denial of emotions that rode so close to the surface. The wind blew harder, biting into the thick, insulated coveralls. If she was already this cold, how would they ever survive the night?

Once again, CJ scanned the rocks for Brad. When she spotted him coming back to the wreckage, she breathed a sigh of relief.

Brad returned with a broad smile, as if he'd done nothing more strenuous than to check them into the nearest hotel. "There's a place over there where two rocks lean together. Right behind that is solid rock. It's not a cave, but very nearly. We could probably use the blanket to block the wind and scoot up under the overhang."

It sounded hopeless to CJ, but she grabbed the blankets and bags while Brad took the first-aid kit and some emergency lights he'd found earlier in the plane. Silently they made their way to the refuge he'd found.

Finding that the mountain tundra yielded little in the way of wood, they used pieces of the plane to stake up the blanket and ward off the wind. Crawling inside, the space proved wider than Brad had originally thought and offered a decent escape from the snow that had started to fall.

CJ rubbed her aching fingers and tried to keep her teeth from chattering too loudly. She played a game with herself of trying to imagine things that were warm. Warm baths, hot towels right out of the dryer, electric blankets—nothing seemed to help.

"I don't think the temperatures will drop too much, but we have to stay dry and warm. We can snuggle up here and do both," Brad said, tossing the remaining blanket around them. "What a hardship."

CJ refused to be humored. "Will they start looking for us

right away?"

Brad shook his head. "They can't in this weather. They'll have to wait it out until it clears. That could be hours or days."

"We could be dead by then."

Brad shook his head. "CJ, I don't think God brought us through the crash just to let us die on this mountain. Where's your faith?"

"I lost it at about twelve thousand feet," she replied seriously.

Brad put his arm around her, and CJ scooted close to avoid him hurting himself by pulling her. "Don't be angry at God, CJ. It won't change a thing, and it'll leave you miserable and bitter."

"Get real, Brad!" she exclaimed, pushing away. "Don't you ever get upset? Don't you ever question why God let something happen?"

Brad looked thoughtful. "Sure. When things like this happen, I ask plenty of questions. But I know that sometimes I don't get to know all the details. We're sitting here in the middle of a mountain, survivors of what could have been a fatal airplane crash, and I can't help but wonder how this works into Romans 8:28."

"Romans what?" CJ questioned with a raised brow.

"Romans 8:28. 'And we know that in all things God works for the good of those who love him. . .' I have a questioning mind, just like you do. Nevertheless, here we are." He looked down at her with a mischievous grin and added, "Alone."

"Brad, how can you joke at a time like this?"

"It beats the alternative."

"Which is?" CJ questioned.

"We could cry. We could lament the situation until our faces turned blue."

"That wouldn't take long. Our faces are already blue from the cold," grumbled CJ. She eased back into Brad's arms, needing to feel his warmth.

" 'Survival is fifty percent attitude, thirty percent mindset, and twenty percent perspective,' a wise man once said." The words sounded familiar to CJ. Brad continued. "In other words, you're going to have to change your way of thinking if you don't want to spend your time up here in misery."

"You talk as though we were at one of your resorts. We're stranded on the side of a mountain. Correction, the top of a mountain. A blizzard is moving in, the temperature is dropping. We're cold, hungry, bruised, and battered. Now I ask you, what part of that should I turn my attention toward in order to get a better attitude?"

Brad shrugged his shoulders. "I guess that would be entirely up to you. Each person finds value in different things. As for myself, I'm grateful we're both alive. It could be very different. I could be standing over your dead body, mourning the loss or vice versa." All trace of humor was gone.

CJ knew he was right. Wasn't that her biggest fear? That had been the reason she was afraid to love him. Fear that he might be taken and she would be left behind had kept her from saying what she really felt. But then, as they were about to face death, she had told him. She wondered if he remembered. As if reading her mind Brad tightened his hold.

"Wait just a minute, CJ. I seem to remember one good thing that came out of this situation."

"What?"

"I recall you telling me something just before we went down. Now, what was it? My mind's just a bit foggy on this. You might have to help me," Brad said, staring up at the rock overhead.

CJ would have elbowed him, but she was up against his

injured side. "I'm sure I don't know what you're talking about," she stated stubbornly and looked away. *So he did remember!*

Brad laughed and brought his hand up to her face, forcing her to look at him. "Did you mean it?"

CJ grew serious. The warmth in Brad's eyes was too much. The feel of his hand on her face was more than she could bear. Emotions welled up and threatened to flood her mind and soul. "Yes," she confessed in a whisper. "I meant it with all my heart. I love you, Brad."

"It took you long enough to admit to it," he said rather dryly.

"I know," she said, lowering her face against the blanket. "I'm sorry."

"Don't be," he replied, his voice low and husky. "I knew what you felt for me, but I also knew you needed time to admit it to yourself."

An uncomfortable silence fell between them as the wind howled outside. CJ didn't know what else to say. What could she say that could possibly explain the way she felt. It was all so new to her. It left her feeling helplessly out of control, a feeling she hated. It was all a matter of attitude, Brad had told her.

"Who was the wise man you quoted a minute ago?" CJ questioned softly.

"Douglas O'Sullivan," Brad replied without looking at her.

CJ nodded and grew quiet again at the mention of her father.

Brad didn't push her to talk. He was content to just sit and wait for her to feel like telling him her thoughts. Closing his eyes, Brad saw the crash again in his mind. The loss of altitude, the mountainside coming up fast. The certainty of death as it loomed before his eyes. No wonder CJ had struggled through the years.

Shaking off the image, he tried to concentrate on what they should do next. CJ wiggled down against his shoulder, breaking all thoughts of their predicament. Instantly, the realization of her body sitting next to his, dependent upon his for warmth, caused Brad's heart to pound. They were as isolated as people could get. Whatever might happen, or not happen, would be a matter of determination and willpower, he quickly realized.

CJ's voice came in a soft, childlike tone. "I've never been in love before," she admitted.

Brad was surprised at the statement and instantly took interest. "Never? Come on, surely there was some sweetheart of a boy way back there, somewhere."

"Nope. Nobody measured up to my standards," CJ said flatly.

"Which were?"

CJ felt her face flush. "You'll laugh at me."

"No, I won't. I promise. I'm just curious to know what standards you hold. Especially if I made it within their tight boundaries."

CJ shook her head and refused to look up. "I wanted a guy like my dad."

"That's quite a compliment. I thank you."

"I suppose," she said, barely breathing the words, "that it's quite strange to be twenty-one and know nothing of falling in love, but it's the truth. Nobody else even interested me. Not in college or even after that. You're the first one." She couldn't take her eyes away from his.

"And the last," he whispered hoarsely before lowering his lips to hers.

CJ's heart raced and her stomach knotted, but this time it was a good feeling. She felt her fears slip away as Brad's kiss deepened. All she wanted to do was forget everything that had happened—the accident, her parents, everything. She began kissing him back with a passion she'd not known existed. She hoped the kiss would go on forever and she wrapped her arms tightly around Brad's neck.

Suddenly, with a noise that was something between a growl and grunt, Brad pushed her away. CJ felt hurt and almost afraid. Brad's frowning face didn't help. With all that she'd endured that day, she couldn't stop her tears from flowing. She sobbed softly into her hands and lay down, turning away so that he couldn't see her cry.

Brad stared down at the crying woman. Why had he done that? Why had he allowed his passions to rule his thinking? Now he was hesitant to even touch her, yet he couldn't leave her in tears. Brad reached out and pulled CJ up. He forced her to sit next to him and brushed her hands away from her face. "I'm sorry," he whispered. "I should never have started that. I don't have much willpower when it comes to you."

"What are you talking about? You told me back at your house that I was always safe with you."

Brad smiled. "You are, but I'm only human. I've wanted to take you in my arms a million times. I've wanted to hold you and caress you and much, much more. Every time you look at me with that helpless, lost expression, I just want to wrap you up and love you." He paused, taking in her surprised expression. "Does that shock you? Have I lost my cape?"

"Your what?"

"My cape. You know. . .Superhero Brad. Didn't you think I was capable of flaws?"

CJ finally smiled. "I guess I was beginning to wonder. But, if being over-passionate is your only flaw, I guess I can manage."

Brad laughed. "Over-passionate and overwhelmed," he said, leaning back against the rock. "When it comes to you, I don't always react the way I should. A man has his limitations. Sometimes my mind drifts off and, well, never mind."

CJ reached out and placed her hand on top of Brad's. "I'm sorry. I should have resisted, but with all of this," she paused, shaking her head, "I just didn't care what happened. I figure if God wants to throw me out here like this, He doesn't care, either."

"That's not true CJ, and you know it. You've got to end this and let go of your anger."

CJ felt her defenses go up. "For what purpose?" she questioned softly and pulled away. "I've tried it and God rewarded me with this."

seventeen

Brad wanted to say something more, but CJ had obviously ended the conversation. He'd never met anyone who held so much anger inside, and it bothered him more than he could say. All he'd wanted to do was help her to recover her life. Now, it was almost as if they were back at step one, and Brad was uncertain he had the strength to go through it all over again.

The storm held on throughout the day, and as the light diminished, Brad pulled out emergency lights he'd brought from the plane.

"We'll only use these if we absolutely need to," he said, giving one to CJ. "There's no telling how long we'll have to wait to be rescued."

The shadowy light inside their shelter made it difficult to make out any features on her face, but Brad knew from her stilted silence that CJ was still upset. All at once, he remembered the breakfast the hotel had packed for them that morning.

"You know, we've been sitting here hungry, and I completely forgot the food we brought from Jackson. I'll go scrounge around the plane and see if I can find it."

"You're going out there?" CJ asked weakly.

"It's only thirty, maybe forty feet away, and you have a light. I'll be right back," Brad answered.

"I could come with you," she offered.

"And have both of us get wet and cold? No, stay here. I'll

need your warmth when I get back."

Crossing her arms in frustration, CJ said no more and waited alone while the wind roared across the valley. She shivered, realizing that two bodies together had produced much more heat than one alone. "Please hurry, Brad," she whispered. She started to feel the odd sensations of her claustrophobia return.

"Why are You doing this to me, God? I've tried to do exactly what I thought You wanted. I've tried to work through the past, and I didn't give in to defeat. What more do You want from me? Why must I suffer again? What is it that I'm not doing that You still expect?"

The wind calmed, and the silence seemed deafening. CJ pulled her knees up and rested her head against them. Why must she always battle against God? For such a wonderful, short time, she'd really thought she had come to terms with her anger and bitterness.

Minutes passed and still Brad hadn't returned with the food. CJ rocked back and forth, trying to comfort herself. She began to hum a song absent-mindedly and suddenly realized it was a praise hymn she'd learned at Bible study. Rejecting the solace it offered, CJ took a deep breath and leaned back in the dark.

Without the wind's constant pummeling, she could hear Brad's approach before the blanket was pulled back. He shined the light right into her face as though she were a criminal being confronted in a dark alley.

"Surprise," he said humorously. CJ didn't laugh.

"I was beginning to think you'd hiked out of here," she muttered and hid her face.

"Nah," he answered and hurried to resecure the blanket. "I found some of the food, though. Oh, and look, the thermos of coffee. It's not pilot coffee, but it's pretty good."

He left the light on and poured some of the liquid into the thermos lid. "It's even a little warm. It'd make a great commercial for the thermos company." Donning an announcer's voice, Brad held up the thermos in an advertising manner and began his mock spiel. "This thermos survived a tragic air crash and, after sitting in the snow-covered wreckage for an unbelievable twelve hours, it amazingly managed to keep the coffee warm!"

"Very funny," CJ said, taking a sip.

"Well, I try," Brad replied. "It took some doing, but I managed to find the donuts, although I think they're frozen solid, and look, here's some packets of jelly! I figure there must be toast somewhere in the plane, but I didn't see it."

CJ took one of the offered donuts and wondered silently if they'd starve to death eating packets of jelly without toast before someone had a chance to find them. Brad seemed unconcerned.

"Shouldn't we ration this stuff?" she finally asked, staring at the donut in her hand.

"Sure. Eat half now and the other half after that." CJ frowned at his joke. Brad just shook his head. "Look, I've a real good feeling about this. I just know that we'll be rescued soon. Where's your faith and trust?"

Indeed, she wondered. *Where is my faith?* She munched on the donut without giving him a reply. Before she knew it, the meal was gone and Brad was sharing a cup of coffee with her. Still she said nothing.

The wind picked up again, and CJ shivered. The temperature had dropped dramatically, or at least it felt that way. She was thankful for the wool sweater and tee shirt she wore beneath the coveralls. Opening her bag, the only other thing CJ found that could help stave off the cold was her other sweater, which she pulled on over the coveralls.

Feeling at odds with the world, CJ concentrated on keeping warm. When other thoughts filled her head, she systematically pushed them aside and refused to deal with them. But perhaps the hardest thing to ignore was the man sitting beside her. He stared at her from time to time and then, just when CJ feared he'd want to start a conversation, he eased himself down on the ground, turned off the light, and went to sleep.

CJ stared down at where she knew Brad rested in the dark. A weary feeling washed over her, but she remained fixed to her spot, contemplating the situation. Surviving the cold required them to share their body heat, but CJ wondered what might happen. How could she just casually sleep beside him. and not be overcome by her feelings?

Realizing that her emotions frightened her, CJ wondered what she should do. If she stayed where she was, they both might freeze to death, and if she joined him, well she couldn't even put words to mind to tell what she was thinking.

What if they don't find us? CJ suddenly realized that living through this crisis was very important to her. She didn't feel the same apathy she had experienced after her parents' crash. She wanted to survive. Her stomach churned. The darkness frightened her more than she could admit.

"Brad," she whispered, not really wanting to wake him, but hoping he wasn't asleep.

"Umm?" His groggy response made her instantly sorry for the disturbance.

"What if they don't come?" CJ realized her question sounded more like a child's whimper.

"They'll come," he answered more clearly.

"But what if they don't? What if the storm doesn't let up? What if we have to stay here for a long time?"

She could hear him sit up and then she felt his hand

touching her arm. "Come here," he ordered, and CJ hesitated.

"I don't think I should," she replied. "I mean, I feel. . . well, I mean. . .remember earlier."

"Hush and come here," he insisted more gently than before. He pulled CJ to him, then touched her face with his. His mouth was up against her ear, his breath was warm.

"Everything is going to work out. You'll see," he whispered. "Now stop fretting and let's get some sleep."

"But, Brad," she started to protest.

"I'm not going to get carried away, if that's what worries you," Brad replied.

CJ felt her heart pounding harder. She couldn't keep from replying, "What if it isn't you I'm worried about?"

Brad chuckled softly. "Got it bad for me, eh?"

"Ohhh!" CJ nudged him away, but he held her fast.

"Look, I got it just as bad for you, but we know what we have to do and we know what's right and what's wrong. Now, let's get some sleep, and I promise to be a perfect gentleman and," he whispered against her ear, "I'll make certain you remain a perfect lady."

Still embarrassed at having told Brad her concerns, CJ settled stiffly into his arms, relishing the warmth as he tucked the blanket around them. She lay straight and rigid, every nerve in her body taut.

"You can't sleep like that," Brad said and yawned. He seemed completely unconcerned. Outside, the wind roared over the mountain like a lion, and CJ reflexively nestled her face against Brad's chest.

"That's better," he chuckled. "Sometimes we just need a little motivation."

In moments, Brad's rhythmic breathing told CJ he was asleep, and although she would have thought it impossible,

CJ finally managed to do the same.

Curled up next to Brad, she tossed and turned, reliving the crash. The scene changed abruptly and faded into the old nightmare. Falling from the sky, CJ could see her parents' stunned faces.

CJ whimpered in her sleep, rousing Brad. He didn't know if it would be better to let her go on dreaming or wake her up. Before he could make a decision, CJ began to cry out. Brad put a hand out to shake her just as she sat straight up and screamed.

Brad reached out and took hold of her. "CJ, wake up. It's only a nightmare."

"Oh, Brad, God must hate me!" she sobbed and fell against him in the dark.

"CJ, you've got to get a hold of yourself. God doesn't hate you. I've been trying to tell you over and over, God loves you. He sent His Son to die for you. Do you honestly think He'd walk away from you with an investment like that?"

"But I've walked away, or maybe I never even knew Him," CJ moaned. "In my dream I—"

"It's the anger inside," Brad interrupted. "Maybe this is what you've got to see, once and for all. The anger you have toward God is eating you alive. It's driving you away."

"But He killed my parents."

"No, He allowed them to die and go home to heaven."

"It's the same thing," CJ wailed.

"No, it's not. Satan is benefiting by the walls you've erected, not God. Satan wins if you walk away," Brad stressed. "God loves you, CJ. I love you. I want you to marry me and share a future together, but not until you've settled this thing."

"But I'm so afraid," she whispered, choking back her tears.

Brad turned on the light. "We get scared in the dark. You're in the dark, CJ. Move toward God and you move into the light."

"Help me, Brad. Pray with me. I want to be free of this. I need to let go of my parents and truly accept God."

After that, sleep came easily, and CJ had no more dreams. She'd made her peace with God, and this time she knew it was real. She wasn't using God as a crutch or even as a way to get to her parents. She had given herself in full to the love that He offered. Things might get rough from time to time, but this time she kept nothing back to accuse Him of later on.

❧

Morning came with a calm and stillness that matched CJ's internal peace. She felt energized and alive. Waking up in Brad's arms seemed to be the most natural thing in the world, and she was hesitant to move. Suddenly, she remembered his words the night before. In a strange but significant way, he'd declared his desire to marry her.

CJ traced her fingers lightly upon Brad's stubble-lined jaw, then placed a light kiss upon his cheek. "I think Daddy would have liked you," she whispered. "I know I sure do." She reached up and pushed back brown hair that fell across his forehead in little-boy style. His even breathing continued, prompting CJ to go on. "You are the bravest and most handsome man in the world, and I love you." She placed another kiss on his cheek. "And you're mine. . .all mine."

Slipping silently from Brad's sleeping form, CJ scooted back against the rock and smiled smugly to herself.

"You look like the cat who caught the mouse," Brad whispered. He surveyed her through barely opened eyes.

CJ jumped. "You ought to warn a person when you do that."

"Do what?" he questioned, easing himself up on one elbow.

"Spy on them." She blushed, knowing that he'd heard every word she'd said while thinking he was asleep. When would she ever learn to keep her mouth shut?

"Good spies don't announce their missions," Brad replied, giving her a mischievous wink. His grin made her blush even more.

"That wasn't nice," she said, trying to focus on anything but him.

"Maybe not, but it was certainly satisfying to hear you stake your claim."

CJ couldn't stand it, and buried her face in her hands, peeking through her fingers. "I can't believe you let me go on. I'm going to remember this moment."

Brad laughed at her discomfort. "I certainly hope so. I know I intend to." He struggled to sit up and winced at the soreness in his side.

CJ immediately lost her self-consciousness and came to help him. "You'd better let me check that out," she said, motioning to his side.

"What? Can't keep your hands off of me now that I'm yours?" Brad teased. He unzipped the coveralls and, with a groan, eased his arm out of the sleeve. CJ helped him with the coat he wore beneath the coveralls and pulled his shirt free from his jeans.

"Now lie down on your side," she ordered, reaching for one of the lights.

"It could just wait," Brad said, sounding less than enthusiastic.

"Just do it, or I'll take back what I said about your being brave."

Brad did as he was told and let CJ poke and prod. Using snow, she cleaned the injured site as well as she could, and when she was convinced she could do no more, she bandaged the wound and allowed Brad to redress.

"I think you'll live," she said, putting things back in the first-aid kit. "You're going to need some stitches when we get back."

"So now you finally believe that we're going to make it?" Brad asked, zipping up the coveralls.

CJ laughed at the way he'd backed her into admitting her hopefulness. "I guess I do."

In glaring white light, Brad crawled out from under the rock and got to his feet. "A rescue team should be able to maneuver now," he declared, "but they'll be hard pressed to see us. The ELT will narrow it down for them, but we can make spotting our site much easier. Let's dig out and throw a little color around this white."

"What about breakfast?" CJ said, reaching for the thermos. "There's still some coffee."

"Cold coffee and frozen donuts. Yum!" Brad exclaimed and threw her a wink.

"You could always go look for the toast," she offered.

Brad reached in and pulled CJ to her feet. "I've got a better idea. First, you kiss me on the lips instead of the cheek and second. . ." His words fell away as he kissed her. He pulled back just a bit, causing CJ to open her eyes. "Never mind about second." He kissed her again.

CJ pushed him back, nearly sending him into the snow. "Oh no you don't. Ever since I met you, you've been feeding me. Now when I'm really hungry, you won't let me eat."

Brad chuckled. "You win. You win." He threw up his hands and turned her toward the half-buried plane. "Good thing we camped close, or we might not have found it. Looks like it snowed pretty good last night."

CJ nodded, squinting against brilliant light. The snow had placed a shroud over the face of the mountain, while overhead the sky was an incredible shade of blue. Moving out, she plunged into the powdery drifts with Brad close at her side. They cleared the snow from the plane and laid out all their belongings that contrasted the most with white to form an X on top of the snow.

That job done, CJ was overcome with a sense of mischief. When Brad wasn't looking, she hurriedly rolled a snowball into her hands and hurled it at his smiling face just as he turned to ask her something.

Plop! The snow broke up, mostly in powder, with just enough wetness to cling to his stubbly chin.

"So that's the game you want to play." His words sounded as though he were answering a challenge.

CJ began to back up. "Now, Brad," she said with a laugh, "remember your side. You don't want to start bleeding again."

"Then you'd better make it easy on me," he said, reaching for a handful of snow.

CJ waved her hands to hold him back. "You wouldn't."

"Oh wouldn't I?" Brad advanced with the snow until he'd backed CJ up against the plane. Glancing down at his hands, he spoke. "It wouldn't be very nice to rub your face in this, would it?"

Feeling reprieved, CJ sighed. "No, it wouldn't."

Brad looked up, and CJ knew by his roguish grin that she'd been had. "But it sure will be fun." The words were no sooner out of his mouth than CJ's face met with a handful of snow.

Batting the wetness out of her eyes, she started to reach down for another handful, but Brad stopped her. He kissed her lightly on the lips, then kissed each of her eyes. "Remember my weakened condition," he teased.

CJ wrapped her arms around his neck. "Be glad I'm compassionate," she murmured.

Brad laughed and, after another brief kiss, released her.

"I'm going to melt some snow. We need to drink plenty of water," he said. "You can get dehydrated pretty fast up here."

"I'll see if I can find anything useful in the plane."

CJ searched through the plane for anything that would offer them further help or comfort. With a laugh, she found the toast plastered alongside the radio, bits of frozen paper still clinging to it in shreds. Still laughing, she called Brad to inspect it.

Brad stuck his head inside and saw the mess of bread that had somehow managed to get entwined with the dash controls.

"Well that confirms it," he said with a grin.

"Confirms what?"

"The radio's toast."

"Oh, Brad," CJ moaned and rolled her eyes. "That's pathetic."

He shrugged his shoulders and reached out to peel off the mess. "Where's that jelly?"

eighteen

The day warmed marginally, making it easy to maneuver around the small area that Brad deemed safe. He reminded CJ that they knew very little of the terrain beneath the snow and that it would be easy to fall into a hole or miss a step.

Brad surveyed their meager supplies, while CJ kept watch on the skies and periodically murmured a prayer. Their prayers were answered when search teams flying overhead spotted them. CJ was more than a little anxious about the rescue, but those concerns faded whenever she thought of Brad's proposal. A proposal that hadn't really been issued.

They gathered their things and waited while the rescue teams decided the best course of action. CJ had hoped Brad would bring up the idea of getting married, but so far he'd kept their conversation light and humorous. Had he changed his mind? Were his words only spoken in the heat of the moment?

Finally she could stand it no longer. The thundering sound of a helicopter overhead caused CJ to glance up from where she sat. A man in bright coveralls and helmet was lowering something down from the open door of the helicopter.

"Looks like we're about to be rescued," Brad said, motioning upward as though CJ had missed it.

It took CJ only a moment to note that the man was now being lowered down, as well. He was strapped to the rope in some strange concoction of lines and was motioning Brad and CJ to stay put.

The man landed several feet from them and shouted, "You okay?"

Brad pulled CJ with him and replied. "Minor injuries, nothing else. Sure glad to see you guys."

The man nodded. "I'll take the lady up first, then come back down for you. You can give us the details later."

CJ inwardly panicked as Brad handed her over to the man and helped him strap her to the line.

"Yes." She stated the word as though he'd just asked her a question, and Brad could only shake his head.

"Yes?" he asked curiously and stepped back. He noted the mischievous grin on CJ's face and raised a brow to emphasize his confusion. "Yes, what?"

"Yes, I'll marry you," CJ stated with a smug expression.

"Oh really," Brad said, crossing his arms against his chest while the rescuer finished checking the line.

"That's right," she replied, refusing to give up.

"I don't remember asking you," he stated blankly. His pretense at seriousness didn't put CJ off for a minute.

"Then you better get to asking, because I might not say yes after we're rescued, and it looks as though I'm about to leave."

Brad laughed. "You drive a hard bargain."

"I might say the same. Sometimes I think you planned all of this," she said, waving her arms to indicate their predicament, "just so you could have me to yourself."

"We're going up. Put your arms like this and hold tight," the stranger told her, and CJ turned with a shrug to Brad.

Brad quickly knelt in the snow. "CJ, you're my dearest friend. You mean more to me than my own life does. Will you marry me?"

Tears came to CJ's eyes, but she didn't care. Rising above the ground, she smiled down at Brad. "Yes!" she shouted down. "Yes, I'll marry you!"

❧

Denver never looked so good, and even though they were forced apart for an observation stay at the hospital, CJ and Brad were clearly bonded for life.

Cheryl arrived to make certain they were both really alive. "The nurse told me you were fine. Is that true?" Cheryl asked in that motherly tone of worry that CJ remembered from long ago.

"I'm great. A little frostbite, but other than that, perfect health. Brad, on the other hand, has twenty stitches in his side. The doctor said it wasn't anything to worry about, though."

"I was so afraid," Cheryl told CJ. "I even insisted Daddy make his friends step up the search. I hassled them so much, I think they thought I was crazy. . .at least Stratton did."

"Stratton?" CJ questioned from the confines of her bed. "Are things any better between you two?"

"I think so," Cheryl said, rather hesitantly. "We've reset the wedding for Valentine's Day."

"You don't sound too thrilled about this," CJ observed suspiciously.

"Well, it's a long story," Cheryl replied. "Let's just say I'm not sure I'm comfortable with everything in our relationship."

"Meaning what?" CJ frowned.

"Meaning," Cheryl hesitated, "that it's a long story. Anyway, I'm glad you and Brad are all right."

"We're more than that," CJ said, forgetting her worry about Cheryl's situation. "We're engaged. He asked me to marry him and I said yes."

Cheryl's face lit up. "CJ! That's wonderful! Have you set the date?"

"No," CJ replied, "but knowing Brad, he won't give me much time. He likes things to move forward at a steady pace."

Cheryl nodded. "Yes, he's always struck me as rather insistent. When do you leave the hospital?"

"Tomorrow, and not a minute too soon. I thought people were supposed to rest while in the hospital. I've been poked, stuck, questioned, and hassled ever since being assigned a bed."

Cheryl laughed. "Don't worry. I'll keep them all at bay once you're back home. Good thing I moved in, eh?"

"Yeah, I'm glad you did. I just wish I'd been a better roommate."

Cheryl shook her head. "You've been great, CJ. You've had a lot to deal with, and now it's over. Now your life really begins."

&

The next day, safe in her appartment, CJ was still thinking about Cheryl's words. Sitting next to Brad, CJ sighed and knew the words were true. It was the beginning. Pressing closer she whispered, "I'm going to like being married to you. You're comfortable in all the right spots."

"Comfortable, eh?" Brad replied against her hair. "I hope that's a good thing."

"The best," she said, pulling back a bit. "At the very least a very redeeming quality." With a sigh, she fell back. "I'm so happy."

"That reminds me, when are we going to set the date?"

"How about now? You are, after all, a person who likes to get things done."

Brad laughed and pulled her into his arms. "How about the first of December? Will that give you enough time to plan all those important girl things?"

CJ giggled, sounding very much like a little girl. "I suppose. Will it give you enough time to plan those boy things?"

Brad's smile was nearly a leer. "I guarantee you it will. In fact, if you want, we can just tie the knot tomorrow down at the courthouse. We boys don't need much time to plan."

"Oh, no, you don't. I want it all. I want the church wedding. I want you in a long-tailed tuxedo. I want to wear a gorgeous wedding dress, and I want a wonderful reception at Denver's finest resort hotel," CJ announced in a breathless manner.

Brad shook his head with a chuckle. "Now who's the organized planner? I'd say you've been thinking about this for quite some time. Just when did you decide we were getting married?"

CJ looked up at the ceiling with a sheepish grin. "Probably when I found out you could be so helpful when I got sick. You've got to love a man who'll hold your hair out of your face while you lose your breakfast."

"How romantic," Brad replied. "Here I thought you'd say something like how you planned to marry me the first moment you looked into my eyes."

"Well," CJ paused, "that might have influenced my decision."

"Whatever influenced it," Brad whispered against her ear, "I'm most grateful. I love you so much, I can't even remember the time when you weren't a part of my life."

"I can," CJ responded softly. "And I'd just as soon never remember it again."

❧

The following morning, CJ woke up before sunrise and, taking her portable phone, she went out on the balcony with a cup of coffee and dialed her brother's number.

A groggy-voiced Curt answered the phone. "This better

be good," he said instead of hello.

CJ laughed. "Well, good morning to you, too. I figured by your time back east, you'd be up and around. Sorry if I misjudged."

"CJ!" he was instantly awake. "I got your message just today. I heard about the crash, too. You okay?" His voice held the same concern Cheryl's had. Perhaps they were both worried that another crash had sent CJ over the proverbial edge.

"I'm fine. In fact, I'm better than that. Curt, I've wanted to talk to you for so long. I've put the past behind me, and I've dealt with the crash. Both of them, in fact," she continued. "God's really been patient with me."

"I'm sorry I wasn't there for you," Curt said, surprising CJ. Then he went on to explain. "After Mom and Dad were killed, I should have stayed with you. I'm really sorry."

"I know," CJ replied softly. "You couldn't deal with it any better than the rest of us. Cheryl told me how hard it was on you, and I guess I just never thought about it, what with my own traumas. It worked out for the best, anyway. God knew just what I needed, or maybe I should say, who I needed. That's the other reason I called. Curt, I'm getting married."

"Brad?" he questioned.

"Yes. He's everything Daddy and Mom would have wanted in a son-in-law but, more importantly, he's everything I want in a husband, and he loves me."

Curt was quiet for several minutes before he finally said, "I'm glad, kiddo. I really am."

"You'll come to the wedding, won't you?"

"Sure, just tell me when and where," Curt replied.

"The first of December at a little church here in Denver."

"I'll be there," Curt promised.

nineteen

CJ was a nervous wreck. She had less than two hours to finish running from one end of Denver to the other. There was still so much to do. She had to make it to the florist before four o'clock in order to confirm that her bridal bouquet was finally to her specifications.

Grimacing, she could still see the dreadful arrangement that had originally been presented to her. It was nothing like what she had ordered. The florist had pulled out her order ready to do battle, but quickly saw her mistake and apologized, promising to have the bouquet redone in time for CJ's last-minute examination.

A quick glance at the car clock caused CJ to step on the accelerator. When her cellular phone rang, she nearly jumped out of her skin. The cell phone had been Brad's idea, and CJ still wasn't used to it.

"Hello?"

"Twenty-six hours, forty-five minutes, thirty-seven seconds and—"

"I get the idea," CJ laughed. "And you're wrong. It's only forty-two minutes, not forty-five."

Brad laughed. "Okay, I stand corrected and quite happily. Where are you?"

"Headed to the florist."

"Gonna make sure they don't mix in red carnations again?"

CJ shuddered. "It really was hideous."

Brad smiled and walked over to the penthouse window. "I can well imagine. Is there anything I can do to help?"

"No," CJ answered as she pulled into the florist's parking

lot. "Not unless you can alter time."

"If I could do that, we'd already be married." Brad's impatience was betrayed in his voice.

"I'm beginning to think we should have eloped," CJ sighed and turned off the engine. "I don't think I have the energy for much more of this wedding stuff."

"Chin up, ol' girl. This time tomorrow—"

"Will be even worse," CJ moaned the words. "Look, I have to run or the florist will close and I'll end up with balloons that say, 'It's a Girl!' floating up from my arrangement."

"Don't let it get you down, CJ. I'll marry you no matter what you end up carrying down the aisle."

"If things get much more difficult, you'll be carrying me down the aisle."

"I can do that, too." Brad was still chuckling as CJ said good-bye.

❧

The hotel's grand ballroom was filled to overflowing with well-wishers, friends, and family. CJ stood beside her new husband and prepared with trembling hand to cut their wedding cake. She looked up at Brad for a moment and smiled.

Brad's eyes met hers, and CJ thought her heart might burst from the happiness she felt. *If only Curt could have been here,* she thought. Something had prevented him from coming at the last minute, however, and though CJ had his promise he'd visit for Christmas, it just wasn't the same. Nevertheless, everything else was perfect, including Cheryl and Stratton, who seemed completely devoted to one another.

CJ felt a deep satisfaction. It was just as she'd planned. The cream-colored satin she'd chosen for her wedding dress was rich and elegant. Styled with a basque waist and sweetheart neckline, the entire bodice was encrusted with tiny seed pearls on lace. The voluminous skirt billowed out around her and ended in a lace inset train that flowed behind her for several feet.

Her thick copper hair had been carefully fashioned with long ringlets cascading down from where the bulk of it was pinned high on top of her head. To this, an exquisite antique lace veil had been attached to trail far behind her like a royal mantle.

Brad, too, cut a dashing figure in his black, long-tailed tuxedo. His cummerbund matched the pale peach gown that Cheryl wore as maid of honor, and the rose in his lapel was the same as the apricot roses in CJ's bouquet. And to her extreme satisfaction and relief, there were no red carnations.

The photographer devoted his attention for the moment to the four-tiered wedding cake. On top was CJ's own special touch—a bride and groom seated in a biplane. Brad thought it especially appropriate and commended her for her ingenuity.

"I didn't know I was getting such a creative wife," he whispered.

"I was going to have the whole cake designed like that mountain you flew into, with us and our little Cessna on top, waiting to be rescued," she teased. Brad started laughing, which drew the attention of everyone.

When the photographer was satisfied that he'd snapped the cake from every angle, he motioned them to go ahead. CJ felt Brad's warm hand cover hers. Together, they drew the knife down through the bottom tier of the wedding cake, while the photographer moved rapidly to capture the moment.

With a grin, Brad raised a piece of cake to CJ's mouth. "Seems I'm always feeding you," he whispered.

"You'd better not get that all over my dress," she replied softly, the smile never leaving her face. "Just remember I get my turn at this."

Brad chuckled and managed to feed her the cake without a single crumb escaping to mar her gown. CJ took her turn, and then they shared glasses of wedding punch. Arms intertwined, bodies touching, CJ and Brad made the perfect couple. After sips of the punch, the crowd around them broke into cheers.

❧

It was two hours later before CJ and Brad could slip away to the penthouse. Knowing the hour would be quite late when the reception concluded, they'd already decided to spend the night at the hotel rather than head out on their honeymoon.

CJ pulled out the pins that held the lace veil and carefully draped the material over the back of a chair. She was married! What a wonder. She'd just committed her life to another human being. It was a responsibility she was only now coming to realize.

She could hear Brad on the phone in his office. Funny how people seemed to know the most inappropriate times to call. CJ walked to the balcony window and pulled back the draperies. All of Denver seemed to be lit up in celebration. Beautiful, she thought. Mesmerized by the twinkling lights, she didn't hear Brad come up behind her. Warm hands touched her neck, soon followed by his lips.

"Ummm," she sighed. "I could get used to this."

"You'd better," he replied. "I think it will be one of my favorite pastimes." Brad turned her around and lifted her in his arms.

CJ wrapped her arms around his neck. "No more phone calls?"

"I turned the phone off," Brad replied.

"What about the maid service?" she grinned.

"I hung the 'Do Not Disturb' sign on the door, and I informed the elevator attendant that no one was to be allowed up to the penthouse until I said otherwise."

CJ giggled. "My husband, the planner."

Brad's lips curled upward in a most mischievous way.

"These are plans that I definitely don't want interrupted."

"Whatever you say, Mr. Aldersson," she murmured, nuzzling her lips to his neck. "Whatever you say."

❧

The sun was already high in the sky when CJ opened her eyes. For a moment she forgot where she was, but the warmth of the man beside her quickly brought back the wonders of the night.

Snuggling closer to Brad, CJ traced a heart on his chest. His hand shot out and closed over her wrist, surprising her. Bringing her fingers to his lips, Brad greeted her.

"Good morning, wife," he whispered.

"Good morning," she replied and leaned up on one elbow, with her hair falling in disarray around her. "I wonder if I'll ever be able to catch you sleeping."

"How's a guy supposed to sleep with someone so beautiful lying next to him?"

CJ laughed and pulled away. "I've got a surprise for you but we have to get out to the airstrip, and look," she said pointing to the window, "we've already wasted half the day."

Brad shook his head. "Are you sure we can't just stay here?"

"Come on," she replied. "I've worked very hard for this surprise."

"Okay," he relented, "but only because I have a surprise out there for you, as well."

❧

The trip to the airport was passed in laughter and conversation of the days to come. They'd decided to fly to a warmer climate for their honeymoon, and because she'd never been there, CJ requested the Bahamas and Brad had readily agreed.

The three-story stone house looked somehow different to CJ. It was her home now. . .hers and Brad's. The very thought filled her with excitement and anticipation.

"I'm so happy," she said, squeezing Brad's arm.

He parked the car and pulled her into his arms. "Me, too," he whispered before giving CJ a long kiss that left her weak in the knees.

CJ melted back against the seat of the Jeep and rolled her eyes. "You sure are good at that."

"Come on," he said with a laugh. "I want to give you your surprise."

They walked hand in hand to a newly built hangar, where Brad came to a stop. "Now close your eyes," he said firmly.

CJ closed them. "All right, I'm ready," she called.

Brad looked over his shoulder for a moment at his wife. She stood there in a long, navy wool coat, copper hair flowing down behind her, and the most innocent look of anticipation on her face. It was definitely hard to concentrate with her looking like that.

Pulling open the hangar doors, Brad stood back. "Okay, you can open your eyes."

CJ did just that and gasped at the newly acquired biplane. "A Curtiss Jenny!" she exclaimed. Her namesake.

"You like it?" Brad asked.

"You know the answer to that. Of course! I love it!" She went to the plane to inspect it. "Oh, Brad, she's lovely." CJ ran her hand along the wing.

"No more so than you," Brad replied. "She's all yours."

CJ turned around with a look of complete shock. "Mine?" She shook her head and added. "Ours. From now on, we're a partnership. Remember?"

"I'll remember. You just remember how much I love you and that for the rest of our lives, I'm going to work very hard to be a good husband."

CJ walked from the plane and pulled something from her pocket. She reached up and handed it to Brad.

"My surprise doesn't seem near as nice," she said.

Brad looked down and immediately recognized the pilot's license. "You're a pilot again?" It was Brad's turn to be astonished.

"Yes, and this time I can fly all on my own, too," she replied proudly. "Although, I'd much rather fly with you."

"How did you manage this and plan a wedding?" he asked curiously.

"You think you're the only planner in this family? We girls can accomplish quite a bit when we put our minds to it. I just thought it would be nice if I could help fly part of the way to the Bahamas."

"I don't know," Brad replied, taking on a doubtful air. "I'm pretty picky about whom I fly with."

CJ laughed and reached her arms up to Brad's neck. Pulling his face down to hers, she whispered, "I bet I can convince you to fly with me." She kissed him long and lovingly, then added, "Does that help?"

"I'm a pretty tough case," he answered. The look in his eyes betrayed his amusement. "I might need a lot of convincing."

CJ laughed and danced away. "Well, I don't," she called back over her shoulder. "I'm flying high and clear. I've married the man I love, and I'm at peace with my God. What more could anyone want out of life?"

Brad easily caught up with her and whirled her around in a circle. "As long as I have you and a wing and prayer," Brad remarked, holding her close, "I have it all."

"A wing and prayer," CJ whispered with a nod. "Now I know Daddy would have loved you."

In the distance the familiar drone of an airplane engine crossed the silence to CJ's ears. It was a good sound, and CJ smiled at the bittersweet memory of another day and time. She was finally free of the past and ready to face the future with a wholeness and happiness of which she'd only dreamed.

"A wing and prayer, Jenny darlin'," she could hear her father say, "are all that you'll ever need."

A Letter To Our Readers

Dear Reader:

In order that we might better contribute to your reading enjoyment, we would appreciate your taking a few minutes to respond to the following questions. When completed, please return to the following:

Rebecca Germany, Managing Editor
Heartsong Presents
P.O. Box 719
Uhrichsville, Ohio 44683

1. Did you enjoy reading *A Wing and a Prayer*?
   ❑ Very much. I would like to see more books
      by this author!
   ❑ Moderately
      I would have enjoyed it more if _____

   _____

2. Are you a member of **Heartsong Presents**? ❑Yes ❑No
   If no, where did you purchase this book?_____

   _____

3. What influenced your decision to purchase this
   book? (Check those that apply.)

   ❑ Cover   ❑ Back cover copy

   ❑ Title   ❑ Friends

   ❑ Publicity   ❑ Other_____

4. How would you rate, on a scale from 1 (poor) to 5
   (superior), the cover design?_____

5. On a scale from 1 (poor) to 10 (superior), please rate
   the following elements.

   ___Heroine   ___Plot

   ___Hero   ___Inspirational theme

   ___Setting   ___Secondary characters

6. What settings would you like to see covered in
   Heartsong Presents books?_____
   _____
   _____

7. What are some inspirational themes you would like
   to see treated in future books?_____
   _____
   _____

8. Would you be interested in reading other **Heartsong
   Presents** titles?   ❑ Yes   ❑ No

9. Please check your age range:
   ❑ Under 18   ❑ 18-24   ❑ 25-34
   ❑ 35-45   ❑ 46-55   ❑ Over 55

10. How many hours per week do you read? _____

Name _____

Occupation _____

Address _____

City_____ State_____ Zip _____

Janelle Jamison

aka. Tracie J. Peterson

The Alaskan Trilogy

___*A Light in the Window*—Julie Eriksson returns to the Alaska territory to begin her career as a public health nurse. Her loneliness and discomfort is compounded by Sam Curtiss who persists in proposing a marriage that Julie fears would end her career. HP56 $2.95

___*Destiny's Road*—Beth Hogan has returned to Alaska a widow and mother of two young boys only to find her village overrun by builders of the Alcan Highway. Beth and her sons grow to love newcomer August Eriksson, but Beth knows she can never marry a man who is fighting God. HP71 $2.95

___*Iditarod Dream*—Mark Williams hopes to become more than Rita Eriksson's coach for the famed Iditarod race, but the walls that Rita has built around herself are too strong for human penetration. HP93 $2.95

Hearts♥ng

HEARTSONG PRESENTS TITLES AVAILABLE NOW:

___HP 37 DRUMS OF SHELOMOH, *Yvonne Lehman*
___HP 38 A PLACE TO CALL HOME, *Eileen M. Berger*
___HP 41 FIELDS OF SWEET CONTENT, *Norma Jean Lutz*
___HP 49 YESTERDAY'S TOMORROWS, *Linda Herring*
___HP 50 DANCE IN THE DISTANCE, *Kjersti Hoff Baez*
___HP 53 MIDNIGHT MUSIC, *Janelle Burnham*
___HP 54 HOME TO HER HEART, *Lena Nelson Dooley*
___HP 57 LOVE'S SILKEN MELODY, *Norma Jean Lutz*
___HP 58 FREE TO LOVE, *Doris English*
___HP 61 PICTURE PERFECT, *Susan Kirby*
___HP 62 A REAL AND PRECIOUS THING, *Brenda Bancroft*
___HP 66 AUTUMN LOVE, *Ann Bell*
___HP 69 BETWEEN LOVE AND LOYALTY, *Susannah Hayden*
___HP 70 A NEW SONG, *Kathleen Yapp*
___HP 73 MIDSUMMER'S DREAM, *Rena Eastman*
___HP 81 BETTER THAN FRIENDS, *Sally Laity*
___HP 82 SOUTHERN GENTLEMEN, *Yvonne Lehman*
___HP 85 LAMP IN DARKNESS, *Connie Loraine*
___HP 86 POCKETFUL OF LOVE, *Loree Lough*
___HP 89 CONTAGIOUS LOVE, *Ann Bell*
___HP 90 CATER TO A WHIM, *Norma Jean Lutz*
___HP 93 IDITAROD DREAM, *Janelle Jamison*
___HP 94 TO BE STRONG, *Carolyn R. Scheidies*
___HP 97 A MATCH MADE IN HEAVEN, *Kathleen Yapp*
___HP 98 BEAUTY FOR ASHES, *Becky Melby and Cathy Wienke*
___HP101 DAMAGED DREAMS, *Mary Hawkins*
___HP102 IF GIVEN A CHOICE, *Tracie J. Peterson*
___HP105 CIRCLE OF LOVE, *Alma Blair*
___HP106 RAGDOLL, *Kelly R. Stevens*
___HP109 INSPIRED LOVE, *Ann Bell*
___HP110 CALLIE'S MOUNTAIN, *Veda Boyd Jones*
___HP113 BETWEEN THE MEMORY AND THE MOMENT, *Susannah Hayden*
___HP114 THE QUIET HEART, *Rae Simons*
___HP117 FARTHER ALONG THE ROAD, *Susannah Hayden*
___HP118 FLICKERING FLAMES, *Connie Loraine*
___HP121 THE WINNING HEART, *Norma Jean Lutz*
___HP122 THERE'S ALWAYS TOMORROW, *Brenda Bancroft*

(If ordering from this page, please remember to include it with the order form.)

Presents

Great Inspirational Romance at a Great Price!

Heartsong Presents books are inspirational romances in contemporary and historical settings, designed to give you an enjoyable, spirit-lifting reading experience. You can choose wonderfully written titles from some of today's best authors like Veda Boyd Jones, Yvonne Lehman, Tracie J. Peterson, Nancy N. Rue and many others.

When ordering quantities less than twelve, above titles are $2.95 each.

Heart♥ng Presents
Love Stories Are Rated G!

That's for godly, gratifying, and of course, great! If you love a thrilling love story, but don't appreciate the sordidness of some popular paperback romances, **Heartsong Presents** is for you. In fact, **Heartsong Presents** is the *only inspirational romance book club*, the only one featuring love stories where Christian faith is the primary ingredient in a marriage relationship.

Sign up today to receive your first set of four, never before published Christian romances. Send no money now; you will receive a bill with the first shipment. You may cancel at any time without obligation, and if you aren't completely satisfied with any selection, you may return the books for an immediate refund!

Imagine...four new romances every four weeks—two historical, two contemporary—with men and women like you who long to meet the one God has chosen as the love of their lives...all for the low price of $9.97 postpaid.

To join, simply complete the coupon below and mail to the address provided. **Heartsong Presents** romances are rated G for another reason: They'll arrive *Godspeed!*